A New Light

A Mount Desert Island Series

Katie Winters

Chapter One

It was New Year's Eve in Bar Harbor. Already, the last of the day's sunlight had begun to dim across the Acadia Mountains, casting the cozy town in grays and pastels. It was the final sunset of another year— one of surprises, family gatherings, babies, weddings, new discoveries, and many, many helpings of delicious food. Kristine, who was now twenty-three and on the brink of the rest of her life, couldn't help but feel nostalgic. Now that she'd made so many decisions about her career, her chosen city, and her romantic partner, there weren't many big, life-shattering decisions left. She was growing up.

Kristine had brought her boyfriend, Patrick, back from New York City to meet her family for New Year's Eve. Patrick drove the rental car, his hands at ten and two, while Kristine sat up front, beaming at him. Behind them, Kristine's twin sister, Bella, was slumped back, nibbling on a piece of chocolate and laughing at something on her phone.

"Bar Harbor looks like a postcard," Patrick said, pausing at a traffic light to take in the quaint New England buildings, the barber shop pole that twisted with red and white, and the red brick library that boasted having been built many centuries ago.

"Right? It's unreal," Kristine agreed, her heart ballooning. It was important to her that Patrick, who was born in New York City, appreciated the little town. It was a part of Kristine's roots, after all.

Kristine and Bella's mother, Heather Harvey, had decided to move to Bar Harbor a little more than a year ago. This surprise move had come in the wake of multiple tragedies, including Kristine and Bella's father's death out at sea. Once in Bar Harbor, Heather had fallen into the mess of her past and learned the truth: that she wasn't the blood relative of either of her sisters, Casey and Nicole, whom she'd grown up with. The truth was much more sinister. Her real mother, a woman named Melanie, had stolen multiple properties and funds from Casey and Nicole's father, gotten involved with another man, subsequently lost those funds, and then sidled Casey and Nicole's father with Heather, her baby with this other man. After Casey and Nicole's father committed suicide, Casey and Nicole's mother graciously raised Heather. Heather called Jane her guardian angel.

Kristine had tried to explain this story to Patrick several times. Each time, he'd shaken his head and said, "This is the craziest, most confusing story I've ever heard. So, you're not related to either of your aunts? And none of your cousins?"

"No. But they're still family," Kristine had said. "Nothing has changed."

"The truth has changed," Patrick had pointed out.

"Bella, are you okay back there?" Kristine turned to catch Bella's eye, as she'd been pretty quiet throughout the drive from the airport.

Bella bit another corner of her chocolate bar and smiled a chocolate-y grin. "Do you think they still have Christmas cookies?"

"At the Keating House? There's no way those stuck around," Kristine quipped.

Patrick pulled the rental into the driveway of the Keating property, snaking past the Keating Inn and Acadia Eatery toward the Keating House. Behind the Keating House, Aunt Casey, an architect, had recently designed and built a new home that resembled the Keating House in design. This allowed multiple "Keating" and "Harvey" people to stay on the grounds comfortably.

"Wow. It's a whole estate," Patrick joked as he turned the engine off.

Suddenly, Heather Harvey stepped out onto the porch of the Keating House, waving her hand excitedly like a child. Her cheeks were bright red from the cold.

"Didn't she just see you guys a few days ago?" Patrick asked.

"She's sentimental." Bella laughed and jumped out of the car, rushing into Heather's arms.

Kristine held back and caught Patrick's gaze. Already, she'd met his family numerous times, as they lived in the city and often invited her to their expensive apartment near Central Park. Their money wasn't like her mother's writing money; it was old, from Europe. Their children went to Harvard and Yale without having to send real applications.

"Are you ready for this?" Kristine teased, wrapping a blonde curl around Patrick's ear.

"As ready as I'll ever be. You know I get nervous out of the city."

Suddenly, the back trunk of the rental burst open. Luke, Heather's boyfriend, called in to say, "Hey, Kris! You going to stay in there all night, or should I bring your suitcase in?"

Kristine cackled, stepped out of the car, and bounded toward Luke, who had almost single-handedly made her mother smile again. Luke laughed and hugged her, then turned to shake Patrick's hand. Patrick and Luke couldn't have been more different. Patrick was wealthy and clean, with a firm grip on the world, whereas Luke had been abandoned by his mother as a young boy and raised in the Ohio foster care system.

Still, Luke and Patrick shook hands in a friendly way. Kristine wondered where her nerves had suddenly come from. Why wouldn't her family welcome Patrick? And why wouldn't Patrick love her family? He'd already told her that he loved her after only four months of dating. That meant something.

Inside the warm glow of the Keating House, Aunt Nicole took their coats while Heather swallowed Kristine, then Patrick, in hugs.

"How was the flight?" Heather asked Patrick, her tone bright.

Patrick shrugged. "Same as ever."

Kristine's stomach tightened. *Why couldn't Patrick have said "good," like anyone else might have?* But Heather laughed and said, "I guess that's a good thing, right? Nothing bad. Nothing good. And you made it on time."

They gathered in the living room, where a large table had been set up. There, the "chefs" of the family, Nicole and Luke, had set up a large variety of party foods. Kristine collapsed on the soft cushions of the couch, warmth from her family's love flowing through her. Patrick selected a single carrot stick and bit the edge before sitting next to her.

"Carrots?" Bella teased him and grabbed a large cracker and a piece of cheese. "I like to end my year with as much good food as possible."

Patrick raised his carrot stick higher. "I like to begin my year with a healthy body."

There was a strange moment of silence, no longer than a couple of seconds. The Keating-Harvey family wasn't one to make anyone feel bad for their opinions; then again, they weren't exactly keen on people who thought they were better than them just because they chose a carrot stick over a slice of cheese.

Still, Kristine loved him. She reminded herself of that. Patrick was different, so different from the people of Bar Harbor. But wasn't that what she wanted? She was now a New York City girl, a woman in the corporate world who knew what she wanted and how to get it.

"I hope you'll try Luke's stuffed pastries," Kristine tried. "They're to die for, and he only makes them once a year."

"Maybe." Patrick crunched through another carrot.

The front door opened, and with it came the sound of Great Aunt Kim's voice. "I smell something delicious!"

Kristine turned to watch as the woman of seventy breezed through the foyer, removing her thick winter coat and her furry hat. Below, she wore a chic outfit— a black turtleneck and a pair of high-waisted jeans. Great Aunt Kim was the older sister of Kristine's real grandmother, the woman who'd abandoned baby Heather during her darkest hour. Against all odds, Great Aunt Kim was a dream. She was kind, considerate, wildly adventurous, and entirely unlike her little sister.

Although Kristine and Bella still didn't know her well, they'd joked about making Great Aunt Kim their stand-in grandmother.

"Aunt Kim, did you really drive that snowmobile over here?" Nicole hustled into the foyer to hug Kim.

"I hope you're careful out there," Casey warned, stepping out of the kitchen.

"Girls, I've been driving a snowmobile since I was four years old," Kim said. "You grew up in Portland. You aren't privy to our ways quite yet." Kim turned her head and winked through the soft glow of the living room directly at Kristine and Bella. "Maybe your daughters aren't too far gone yet."

Heather laughed. "My daughters live in New York City. They're all about fashion and subways. Not snowmobiles."

Aunt Kim swept through the living room to first hug Kristine, then Bella. She looked them dead in the eyes, as though she tried to peer into their soul, and then she dropped her chin to look at Patrick.

"And who is this handsome young man?"

"This is my boyfriend, Aunt Kim. Patrick."

Patrick stood to shake Kim's hand. Kim sized him up, her eyes in slits.

"Have you been to Bar Harbor before, Patrick?" she asked.

"Never. Although I hear it's lovely in the summertime." Patrick spoke too loudly, as though he addressed a whole room.

The corners of Kim's lips curved into an unhappy smile. "We like to think it's lovely all year round."

Suddenly, Grant, Melody, and Donnie entered the living room with a suggestion to play a board game. Kristine breathed a sigh of relief, praying that people would stop analyzing every little thing that Patrick said incorrectly.

"Can I get you a glass of wine?" she asked Patrick. She then grabbed a little pillow and flopped it against his arm playfully. He winced.

"Um. Sure." Patrick stood and followed her into the kitchen. Kristine knew that he hated board games; probably, he just wanted to get away from the action.

In the kitchen, Heather, Casey, and Nicole stood at the kitchen counter, each with a glass of wine raised. Heather's smile was effervescent.

"Honey, I was just telling Nicole and Casey about your new job," she said to Kristine, who uncorked a bottle of red and began to pour. She passed the first glass to Patrick, as he was the guest. "What was the title again?"

"She's the personal branding assistant for Richard Coswald," Patrick answered for Kristine, then took a sip of his wine. "It's a remarkable position. Something that almost every twenty-something fresh out of business school applied for."

"It sounds fantastic," Nicole said. "So important."

Kristine blushed, her eyes to the ground. "Yes. It does sound like that. I only wish that Mr. Coswald was a bit, erm, different?" She stuttered slightly. "I wouldn't call him the most feminist boss. He's said a few things here and there that have made me uncomfortable." She wrinkled her nose, unsure if she should have shared this, especially with her mother.

"Oh no. A man from the old guard," Casey said, shaking her head. "I've worked with many men like that. To be frank, I'm grateful to work for myself and only for myself now."

"It's just what I keep telling you," Patrick chimed in. "Sometimes, you have to force yourself through difficult situations just to get to the ultimate prize. This job will lead to something amazing. I just know it."

Heather gave Patrick a dark look, which she soon rebounded. "Honey, if you don't feel comfortable there, there's no reason to stay."

"No. Patrick's right," Kristine offered, mostly because she wanted him to be right more than anything in the world. She looped her arm through his and smiled at her mother, trying to be grateful for the world she'd built for herself in the city.

"Just tell me that you'll keep tabs on the situation. I don't want you to be unsafe," Heather warned.

"I promise, Mom. I do."

That night, the Keating-Harvey families celebrated a gorgeous new year together. They ate, drank, laughed, played games, and watched the fireworks explode across Frenchman Bay. Slowly, Kristine eased into herself, finding a better rhythm with both Patrick and her family members and frequently making Patrick laugh.

Once, in the kitchen for a refill, Bella grabbed Kristine's arm and said, "Are you really sure about this guy?" But Bella was slightly drunk and clearly in one of her moods. Kristine wasn't willing to give power to it.

"Patrick is wonderful. He's just nervous, being around so many people he doesn't know," Kristine said.

"He acts like he's better than everyone here," Bella shot back.

Kristine rolled her eyes. "You just don't know him very well. We should have dinner in the city soon. You, that guy you're seeing, Patrick, and I." Kristine had forgotten which of the many artists Bella was into at the moment.

Bella shrugged and said, "All right. You're probably right." She then dropped her head on Kristine's shoulder, exhaled deeply, and said, "I'm just so glad I have you, Kristine. And I want you to be happy, no matter what. Okay?"

Kristine's heart swelled with love for her twin. The "twin bond" was a very real thing, something difficult to express to those who didn't understand. Once, when the girls had been ten, Bella had broken her arm across town, and Kristine had woken up from a nap, weeping with fear. Nobody had ever been able to explain it.

That night, Kristine snuggled into bed beside Patrick, who smelled of expensive cologne and toothpaste. She kissed his chest, his cheek, and his lips, and she whispered, "I hope you're happy?"

Patrick, who was already half-asleep, just mumbled, "Happy New Year." It was enough to allow Kristine to continue to believe in their love. Maybe she always would.

Chapter Two

Kim Hyde Robinson was seventy years old, which meant that this New Year's Day was her seventy-first New Year's Day— a fact that should have startled her. Still, nothing much startled her, not after so many years of surprises. There had been good surprises, like the births of her two children and all the love they'd brought her, along with the bad ones, like her parents' early deaths, her little sister Melanie's manipulation tactics, and, of course, her divorce several years back.

Kim awoke at the Keating House, a beautiful colonial that had once belonged to Melanie's ex, Adam. The long and winding road of life was a strange one. She stood at the window and brushed through her long, dyed black hair, gazing out at the sweeping hills, which glittered with snow. It was hard not to feel optimistic on New Year's Day, as though you'd never make past mistakes again. You'd learned better. You were older, wiser.

She dressed in a pair of jeans and a sweater and made her way downstairs, where breakfast bacon sizzled in greasy skillets, eggs cooked, potatoes baked in the oven, and croissants and freshly baked rolls had been placed in the center of the kitchen table, along with a large block of farm-fresh butter. Nicole and Luke were in control of the kitchen and ordered Heather about.

"I see they work you hard around here," Kim teased as she poured herself a mug of coffee.

"They're the kitchen masters. I can't dispute anything they say," Heather said as she continued to slice onions. "If it were up to me, we'd have a nutritional breakfast of cereal and pop tarts."

"She's exaggerating," Nicole said. "Heather is a fantastic cook."

"Heather? She's good at everything. It's annoying." Casey, the eldest Harvey sister, stepped through the kitchen doorway and hugged Kim, having just walked through the snow between the newly-built house and the Keating House. It seemed likely that the families no longer knocked on the front doors before entering, treating the entire property as their own.

"I don't think I could have designed the architectural plans for that beautiful house over there," Heather suggested, locking eyes with Casey. "Good thing we have a world-class architect on our hands."

Kim sipped her coffee, her heart lifting as she fell into the easy rhythm of the Harvey sisters' conversations. Often, when she was with them, she felt a wave of jealousy rise within her. She and Melanie had never been able to enjoy such an easy friendship. In fact, they'd spent most of Melanie's short life not speaking at all.

"So, Heather." Casey sounded conspiratorial as she leaned against the kitchen counter. "What do you think of Kris's new boyfriend?"

A shadow passed over Heather's face.

"Uh oh!" Nicole cackled. "I know what that means."

"Oh, come on. He's fine." Heather tried to backtrack.

"You hate him!" Casey hissed.

"Will you quiet down?" Heather insisted, wiping her hands on a towel. "There's no telling when they'll get up. Patrick is a workaholic city-type. He probably had a business meeting at seven o'clock this morning to get the year started off right."

Nicole, Casey, Luke, and Kim howled with laughter.

"He's certainly not good enough for our Kris," Kim affirmed.

"I wonder what she sees in him?" Nicole asked softly, eyeing the kitchen doorway.

"I see what she sees," Kim quipped with a laugh. "He's handsome. Rich. Probably from a powerful family. I remember those men from my brief time in New York City."

"She'll figure it out," Heather said, furrowing her brow.

"Yeah. I just hope she doesn't take as long as I did to figure out Michael was hot garbage," Nicole said, scrunching her nose. She was the only Harvey Sister who'd gotten divorced, although Casey had separated from her husband, Grant, for a period of time before getting back together.

"Women get married and divorced all the time," Kim said. "Everything in life is a learning experience."

"Oh, gosh. I just hope my darling daughter doesn't have to fall that hard before she learns to stay away from guys like him," Heather said under her breath.

* * *

By noon, the rest of the family members had dragged themselves out of bed and limped to the breakfast table for a feast. Kim sat between Bella and Kristine, young, beautiful women who very much looked like she and Melanie had back in the old days. Next to Kristine, Patrick ate a low-carb breakfast, careful to say no to any piece of toast, biscuit, or pancake that was sent in his direction. Just now, he explained the intricacies of the Keto diet to Luke, who, despite being a very kind man, seemed on the brink of exploding.

"Should we go around the table and talk about our New Year's Resolutions?" Abby, Nicole's twenty-something daughter, asked.

"I think that's a great idea," Nicole said, eyeing her boyfriend, the very rich Evan Snow, who sat beside her. "Who should start?"

"I will." Angie, Luke's biological sister who'd only come into the picture a year or so before, tapped her napkin across her mouth and smiled at her daughter, Hannah, who was a brand-new mother as of late summer. Beside Angie sat her new boyfriend, a drummer named Paul, who played in Angie's jazz band.

It was wonderful to be around, so many different people, all of whom had decided to rewrite the stories of their lives in middle age.

"My New Year's Resolution is to perform at bigger jazz clubs in Portland, Boston, and maybe even New York," Angie said, continuing to smile at her boyfriend.

"And it sounds like you're not that far away from that goal," Heather said. "I read the article about your jazz ensemble in the paper. You've gotten some real attention."

Angie blushed and squeezed Paul's hand over the table.

They continued to go around the table, announcing their resolutions. Heather said she wanted to finish another fantasy novel, which would be published the following year. Nicole said she wanted to be more experimental about the menu at the Acadia Eatery. Hannah and Abby both spoke about growing their photography business, which they'd founded the previous year.

When it reached Kim, she dropped her eyes to her half-eaten eggs and said, "It's funny to be seventy. I've already lived so many beautiful lives. What more could I possibly want?"

Everyone laughed good-naturedly.

"Just say something," Bella urged. "Anything."

"All right. All right." Kim raised her glass of orange juice and said, "My resolution is to hang out with this family a whole lot more. The warmth I've felt in this house over the holiday season has been very important to me."

Heather's eyes glittered with tears. Just like Melanie, Heather was always quick to cry, although Heather's tears were always more sentimental and filled with love, while Melanie's had always been manipulative.

Kristine went next, saying that she wanted to commit to visiting family in Bar Harbor at least once every two months and train for a marathon.

"A marathon! No thanks," Kim teased.

After that, Patrick said, "My resolution is to have only twelve percent body fat and to make an additional twenty-five thousand dollars per year."

Heather's eyes bugged out. For a moment, the table was very quiet, taking in the money-driven and egotistical nature of Patrick's resolution. His had nothing to do with family or love. It disgusted Kim, and she strained not to show it on her face.

The family rebounded easily, as nobody wanted to make Kristine feel too badly that her boyfriend was a complete dud. Very soon, Nicole and Evan were squabbling about who would take the last sausage, Bella was telling Kim about her new series of paintings, which would be shown in a New York City gallery space at the end of February, and Patrick and Kristine were joking easily, their eyes flashing flirtatiously.

Nothing about this day could possibly get them down.

Kim found herself staying at the Keating House for the better part of that afternoon, sipping hot cocoa, walking the grounds with the Harvey Sisters, and playing board games. As the light began to dim across the snow, her daughter, Jennifer, texted to say she planned to make dinner that night for herself and Kim's great-grandson, Oliver. "Let's meet at your place?"

"I've been called back to my little family," Kim announced to the kitchen, where Heather, Nicole, and Casey had just cracked open a bottle of wine.

"Nonsense. You belong here," Nicole teased. "We have plenty of wine and beds to go around."

Kim giggled. "My daughter's cooking, I'm afraid."

"Gosh. And here I was, thinking you thought of us as your daughters," Casey said.

Kim's heart lifted. She'd never anticipated this influx of new love. "Don't tell Jennifer, but sometimes, when she's particularly cranky, I think I might like you three more," Kim said.

Heather, Casey, and Nicole laughed, their hearts open. They set down their wine glasses and insisted on walking Kim out to her snowmobile, which she'd parked to the right of the driveway. With her coat over her shoulders, she waved into the living room, where numerous people turned and said, "Happy New Year, Aunt Kim!"

Kristine and Bella scrambled out of the sea of family members and hugged Kim, knowing they wouldn't see her until they returned to Bar Harbor for another visit.

"I wish you both luck in that crazy city," Kim said, wishing she could impart at least a bit of wisdom, but knowing that she couldn't. "I know things aren't always so kind there. Keep your heads up."

"We will," Kristine and Bella promised just before Kim stepped out into the snow.

Kim felt most at home on a snowmobile. There was tremendous power in the ability to whip out across the rolling hills of snow, with sharp wind in her face. Her teeth were chilled, and the curls outside of her helmet flapped. Her house was a little ways from downtown Bar Harbor, about a half-mile from the shoreline, where the Acadia Mountains began to stretch toward the sky.

The roads from the Keating House to Kim's place were mostly empty, as everyone hibernated within the warmth of their homes, eating leftovers and preparing themselves for another three-hundred and sixty-five days of yet another year. After the warmth of the Keating House and the generous conversations, Kim's heart felt ready for whatever came next.

Maybe she'd even meet someone and have a fling. Maybe she'd finally take up the hobbies she'd always thought she would in retirement. Or maybe she'd finally get into fitness and become one of those little old ladies who ran ultra-marathons across mountains.

The world was open.

The light was fading. Kim turned on the headlights on her snowmobile but refused to slow down. The wind had gotten even chillier in the ten minutes since she'd left, and she was eager to get home and cut out the pain. Besides, she'd taken this route home thousands of times. She knew the road like the back of her hand.

The thing was, no amount of knowing the road could ever account for a drunk driver in a very large pickup truck.

When the pickup's headlights whipped around the corner and began to come right toward her, Kim had to act quickly. She thrust her snowmobile out of harm's way, very narrowly missing the pickup. The driver smashed the horn, as though the potential accident was Kim's fault.

To the right of the road was a very thick stretch of trees. Kim had no longer than two or three seconds to breathe a sigh of relief before she smashed into the thick trunk of a two-hundred-and-fifty-year-old oak and disappeared into her unconscious. There was nothing but darkness.

Chapter Three

It was the middle of January. New York City snow had come and gone, leaving a disgusting gray slush along the sidewalks and edges of the road. Kristine, whose boss had sent her out for a very specific coffee order thirty minutes ago, now hustled in heels through the sludge, her eyes on the automatic doors that would welcome her back into the warmth of the high-rise building. Upstairs, Richard waited for his coffee— and she already knew he wasn't happy with how long she'd been.

"It wasn't my fault," Kristine grumbled at the coffees, which sloshed angrily and burnt her fingers. The line at Richard's favorite coffee place had wrapped around the corner because it had offered some deal on a new marshmallow chocolate chip brownie. When she'd asked Richard if another coffee shop would work for him today, he'd texted back angrily: **JUST DO YOUR JOB.**

In the elevator, Kristine tried to steady her breath. There was nothing worse than gasping in front of Richard, who so often berated her for her lack of fitness. When was she supposed to exercise? Sometime after her fourteen-hour shift? After the short dinner she normally stuffed it into her mouth before she passed out in bed. *When?*

Again, Kristine reminded herself of how lucky she was to have gotten this job at all. As Patrick said, thousands of business students had applied for the position after graduation, and Kristine had been Richard's choice. This was the steppingstone to greatness.

Richard's secretary hissed as Kristine approached. "Where have you been? And why do you look like you ran a marathon to get here?"

Kristine puffed her cheeks. "The line was around the block."

"So? You know what to do, Kristine. You lie. Tell them you're late for a funeral. Anything to get to the front," the secretary said.

Kristine flared her nostrils angrily. Little did this secretary know that Kristine had experienced her fair share of loss and wasn't so keen on lying about a funeral. Her father had died, for goodness sake.

"Just go," the secretary said, waving toward Richard's door. "He has fifteen minutes to go over the next account with you. Let's pray he doesn't take your head off."

Kristine rapped on the door, heard Richard's arrogant, "Come in," and entered. Richard sat behind his desk, studying a print-out upon which Kristine had written every detail that he was required to know for his upcoming meeting with a new client. Last night, Kristine had stayed two hours after everyone else to finish that document, which he now basically threw to the corner of the desk.

"Kristine." He shot her name icily. "When you hear that I need a cup of coffee, do you think to yourself, 'Oh! I have three hours to do that.'"

Kristine's tongue was very dry. "The line was around the block."

Richard waved a hand, uninterested. "Do you know how many people wanted this job, Kristine? How many people would trade their right arm to stand where you are today?"

Kristine bristled but said nothing. She wanted to ask Richard when he would drop the coffee issue so they could get to the task at hand. If Kristine didn't prep him for this next meeting, he wouldn't be ready for it. He would look like a fool.

Kristine placed his cup of coffee on the desk, sat in the chair opposite him, removed her notepad from her pocket, and tapped the edge of her pen against the paper. She looked at him expectantly as though she was the adult, and he was the toddler.

"Victor has a real problem with our initial pitch," Kristine said simply, choosing to ignore his tantrum. "Which is why I've restructured points two through five, as you can see on that document."

Richard coughed and flipped through the document again. "If only I wasn't so tired. Maybe I could make sense of this."

"There's a coffee right in front of you."

"Let's not use such a sharp tone with me, young lady." His eyes glittered menacingly.

Kristine had the insane desire to throw the contents of her coffee cup onto his pristine white shirt. Instead, she righted her smile and said, "As I said, I think Victor will appreciate the slight changes to the narrative. If you follow the script in front of you, I imagine the meeting will go very smoothly. What do you think?"

* * *

Back at Kristine's desk, she dropped her face into her hands and allowed a few tears to fall into her palms. It was important she didn't let her colleagues see her weakness, as that sort of thing was always used against her. Like Richard and Patrick reminded her, everyone wanted her job, and everyone wanted to undermine her. Tears were a woman's thing. She had to be hard like a man supposedly was.

Kristine scanned her emails and was grateful to find her mother had written her not an hour before. Kristine had asked her mother to email her rather than text her, as it meant reading Heather's emails would look more like work.

Kristine,

Hi, honey. I hope you're doing all right. I've just come from the hospital to see Aunt Kim. Unfortunately, she's still in a coma, and the doctors have no idea how long it will last. The longer it goes, the more difficult it will be for her to recover. As you can imagine, Jennifer has been inconsolable. We've had her over to the Keating House a few times for dinner, but it's very difficult to get her mind off the topic of her mother. We all know that Aunt Kim was a wonderful snowmobile rider. Who knows what happened out on that road?

It terrifies me to remember that anything can happen at any time. Please, tell me that you're keeping yourself safe in the city. Please, tell me that you and your sister are taking good care of each other.

I have to admit that I'm not the biggest fan of that boss of yours. You've been quiet about him since New Year's, but I want you to know that I'm here to talk whenever you need to. You were always so driven to meet your goals, but this boss doesn't have to be a "necessary steppingstone" to those goals, you know? Maybe there's no real space for cruelty in the world. There shouldn't be, anyway.

I love you so much,

Mom

Kristine managed to leave the office at half-past seven, at which time she scrambled into the night and hailed a cab to take her to Brooklyn. In the soft darkness of the back of the cab, she texted Bella and Patrick that she was on her way. Bella wrote back immediately to say she and her sort-of boyfriend, Florian, were already there. Patrick didn't write at all.

Kristine's heart thudded slowly. Outside her window, she took in the dramatic contrasts of a city that would always surprise her. People wore haute-couture or else slept in tents under bridges. Kristine and Bella were somewhere in the middle, both hungry with dreams. Kristine was to be a high-powered businesswoman and marry into a powerful New York City family, while Bella wanted to crawl up the ladder of the art world. It was funny where life took you.

Bella and Florian already sat at the trendy restaurant in Brooklyn, there beneath a lime green light, their hands clasped over the table as they chatted joyfully. Kristine's heart lifted, and her shoulders released their tension. She would always feel that way when she saw her twin. It was always like coming home.

"Hi!" Bella jumped up, dropping Florian's hands to hug Kristine close.

"Oh. Hi." Kristine breathed, closing her eyes tightly. "You smell so good! New perfume?"

Bella laughed as their hug broke. "I stole some from Florian's roommate." She furrowed her brows, studying Kristine's face as they sat. "What's wrong?"

"Nothing. Nothing." Kristine waved a hand.

"It's Richard. Isn't it? That idiot. He makes your life a living hell."

Kristine shook her head, not wanting to get into it. "Mom emailed me today. Kim's still..."

Bella nodded, a shadow passing over her face. "I know. She wrote me, too." She then turned to Florian to explain, "Our Great Aunt Kim was in a terrible snowmobile accident on New

Year's Day. We'd just spent the day with her. She's been in a coma ever since."

"That's terrible." Florian stuttered sadly. "Do they know what caused the accident?"

Bella and Kristine shook their heads, both awash with memories of their beautiful great-aunt. Before either of them could think of something to say next, Patrick breezed through the double-wide doors, nodded at a passing waitress, and dropped down to kiss Kristine on the cheek. Kristine found her voice and said, "Hello! How was your day?"

Bella and Florian both exchanged glances, probably about Patrick's swanky suit and his demeanor, which demanded attention and respect. That was okay. That's what this dinner was about, anyway. Kristine wanted Bella and Patrick to learn to like one another. No, that wasn't it. She needed them to like each other. It was one of the most important things in her life.

"I just closed a fantastic account," Patrick said as he sat, rapping his knuckles against the table. "You should have seen me in there. I had complete control over the room. Everyone was eating out of my hands."

Bella and Florian tried to smile.

"That's fantastic, Patrick." Kristine squeezed his arm.

"So, I guess you're well on your way to reaching your New Year's Resolution," Bella suggested, her voice lined with acid.

"Pardon me?" Patrick asked, apparently not remembering what he'd said for his resolution.

"Never mind," Bella offered. She then glanced toward Florian and said, "Florian just got an offer to feature his sculptures in a gallery space here in Brooklyn."

"That's great news!" Kristine said.

Patrick bristled. "Which gallery space?"

"The Pyramid," Florian said proudly.

Patrick dropped his gaze to the menu. "I see."

Florian arched his brow. "Is there something wrong with The Pyramid?"

"No, no. I just know the real money doesn't show itself at that kind of gallery," Patrick said evenly. "But you know. It's a steppingstone to the next thing."

Bella looked livid. "Excuse me? When was the last time you had your art featured in a gallery, Mr. Businessman?"

Patrick laughed. "Art isn't exactly my thing, as you know. Money, on the other hand, is. I'm just saying. Maybe if I had been Florian, I would have waited for a better offer."

"Well, you're not Florian," Bella seethed.

Kristine wrapped her hand tenderly around Patrick's bicep. "Why don't we order some cocktails?"

Bella continued to glare at Patrick, even when Florian whispered for her to "drop it." The waiter soon arrived and took their cocktail orders, along with a selection of appetizers. Kristine reminded herself not to eat too much, as she'd seen a dramatic uptick in respect from Richard since she'd lost about three pounds. She didn't want to lose that respect.

The night continued on, with Patrick finally finding it within himself to ask Bella about her painting series and Florian about his sculptures. Kristine was grateful to fall into the cadence of her sister's words, surrounded by both her love and Patrick's. Later, in the bathroom, when Bella asked her (yet again) if she really thought Patrick was "the one," Kristine bristled and asked, "Isn't he getting better?"

To this, Bella said, "Do you really want to date someone who has to 'get better' when it comes to the way he treats your family?"

"He loves me, Bella. I'm happier than I've been in years," Kristine insisted.

Bella nodded, her eyes wide. It was clear she didn't believe her. Kristine wasn't sure if she believed herself, either.

Chapter Four

Great Aunt Kim's condition remained unchanged. Kristine's mother sent daily updates from the hospital, saying she hoped just talking to Kim aloud would keep Kim in the world somehow. "I tell her how much we love her and need her to come back to us." Kristine's heart went out to her mother; after all, Kim was a new mother figure for Heather, who'd gone through so much heartache and loss over the years. It seemed inconceivable that she would have to lose another mother figure so soon after she'd learned to love her.

The weather in the city was continually grim. Slush continued to pile, and ice shimmered dangerously outside door frames. Shop workers were grumpy, making every interaction alienating. Above all, Richard seemed bent on demanding more and more ridiculous "tasks" from Kristine, who spent the majority of her time ensuring his career didn't go off the rails.

Only twice did she complain about Richard to Patrick. Each time, he convinced her she was the luckiest woman in the world to have this position. "Don't be crazy. You have to hold onto this for the next three years, at least. Besides, I'm sure you're learning a lot."

Toward the end of January, Kristine found herself hard at work on Richard's sixteen-year-old daughter's high school ethics essay. It was essential that his daughter get at least a B+ so she wasn't held back for spring break, during which time Richard planned to take his children to Bora Bora. Kristine had always been a good student and was still proud of some of the essays she'd written as a teenager and college student. Then again, she hadn't pushed herself through four years of business school just to write sentences like: *"Our modern understanding of ethics can help us mold better systems in high schools to ensure more balance and empathy."*

Frustrated, Kristine found herself complaining about the essay to one of her colleagues at the office. "I can't believe I have to write his sixteen-year-old daughter's essay. Like, is she too dumb to do it herself?"

This was Kristine's ultimate mistake. She'd always known people were apt to turn on each other in that office, if only to crawl their way to more power. When Richard called her into the office an hour later, Kristine walked in and was asked, "Do you think you're too good for the very important work I've asked of you? If so, you can find your way out of the building. Now."

Kristine felt as though she'd been slapped. She gaped at him, genuinely surprised, until it dawned on her that she shouldn't have been surprised at all. Suddenly, she lifted her chin and said, "The way you use and manipulate people is very wrong. You should be ashamed of yourself. On top of it all, you have very little comprehension of what goes on in your own field. Without me for the last six months, you would have been lost."

She then turned on her heel and stalked from the building, not bothering to pick up her things at her desk.

Outside, Kristine floated down the sidewalk, no longer noticing the sludge on the sidewalk or the grumpy expressions of the passers-by. She hadn't remembered to grab her coat and had only her wallet, her phone, and her house keys, which was enough. As she went, she felt the horror of what she'd just gone through float off of her. Why had she ever put up with that man? Why had she ever allowed him to ridicule her when she hadn't gotten his coffee order quite right? Wasn't she better than this?

It was nearly seven, and Kristine realized she'd been walking for over an hour. Exhausted, she dropped into a local bar, ordered a beer, and texted Patrick to ask him to meet her. He agreed and appeared about twenty-five minutes later, his brow furrowed.

"Before you say anything, I already know." Patrick slipped into the chair across from her and let his shoulders drop. "And listen, we'll get through this. Together."

Kristine was taken aback at this, as she hadn't felt anything but euphoria since Richard had told her to leave. Still, she was grateful for Patrick's support and thanked him, smiling.

"It was a tough job. Maybe too tough for you," Patrick suggested. "But you'll find something else. You're talented, Kristine. I wouldn't be in this relationship if I didn't think we made a good team."

Kristine's heart lifted. "We do make a good team," she repeated, choosing to fixate on that part of what he'd said. It had been a long time since anyone had wanted to be serious with her. *Wasn't that a beautiful thing?*

That night, she and Patrick drank beers, laughed, and searched online for better jobs for Kristine. They cozied up on his couch, turned on a movie, and held each other as a soft New

York City snow fell outside. Kristine texted her mother about the job change and checked up on Kim, who remained in a coma. Kristine allowed herself to hold all of these emotions at once— sorrow for Kim, gratefulness for her relationship, and hope for whatever future she would build next. Life was a complicated thing. Maybe, at twenty-three, she just wasn't very good at it yet.

Several days later, Kristine watched Bella gather her paints to head to her studio.

"It's weird you aren't at work already," Bella said, clearly giddy about Kristine's change of job.

"I know. I'm living a life of leisure," Kristine joked.

"Seriously. You should enjoy this time off," Bella said. "You've saved up enough for a few months off, haven't you?"

Kristine shrugged. "I'll have this big gap on my resumé. It's awkward."

Bella groaned. "You can't think about your resumé all the time. You have to think about your life. Your happiness. Think of Aunt Kim! Think of Dad." Her eyes flashed. "Their lives were cut short just like that. You have to enjoy the time you have. You can't give any more of it to Richard."

Kristine walked Bella to the door, thanking her for her pep talks. Before she left, she said, "Patrick's actually been a huge help in all of this." She still wanted to paint a picture of Patrick that Bella could get on board with.

"Huh. Finally," Bella said with a mischievous smile. She then dove down the staircase and into the chilly streets, her bags stocked with paintbrushes and paints.

According to the HR department at Richard's office, Kristine had to come in to give an exit interview and collect her coat and other possessions. Kristine decided to take her time getting ready, putting on an extra layer of makeup and selecting a perfect outfit. Hopefully, this was the last time she would see these people. She wanted to look her best.

Kristine left the house early. Sunlight peeked through January clouds, advertising a spring that couldn't come quickly enough. On the way, she stopped for a cup of coffee and a croissant, which she ate slowly, reading the newspaper. It was wonderful to be out in the middle of the day without anything to do. Often, she glanced up and saw young women around her age racing through the streets, on their way somewhere, probably to get coffee for someone who hated them. *What a waste of time.*

When Kristine stepped into the elevator at the high-rise building, a shiver ran up and down her spine, a mix of nerves and memories of anxiety. Kristine thanked her lucky stars she would be able to leave in twenty minutes, maybe thirty tops. Maybe she would grab a matinee screening before Patrick got out of work. They planned to cook dinner together later, something they rarely did, as neither of them had the time to grocery shop. "I have time now, Patrick," she'd told him. "Let's make something complicated and delicious."

The woman at the front desk greeted Kristine curtly, passed over a box of her things, and instructed her to go to meeting room A for the exit interview. Kristine thanked her and entered the meeting room, where an HR rep waited with a clipboard. There, Kristine did her best to illustrate just how poisonous the working environment had been for her throughout the six months she'd worked there.

"He makes you feel like you're disposable," she explained, "even as you know you're doing everything in your power to keep his business afloat."

The HR rep scribbled notes on her clipboard. It was unclear if she wrote what Kristine said or if she just pretended to. Kristine decided she didn't care. She was just grateful to speak like this about Richard, only a few rooms from where he sat.

"I hope you'll warn the next person who applies for my

position," Kristine continued. "Tell them they'll lose their sense of self. That they'll give more of their heart and their mind to this man than anyone deserves."

The HR rep nodded again and clicked her pen. "Thank you, Miss Talbot. I believe that's all we need from you today. Why don't you see yourself out?"

Kristine had been talking for a little more than twenty-five minutes, which suddenly didn't feel like enough time. She had much more to say. Instead of making a fuss, she stood, then grabbed her box of things, and stepped out into the foyer.

There, seated in one of the plastic chairs outside the front desk, was a familiar man.

"Patrick?" Kristine couldn't help but smile. This gorgeous and successful man had chosen her as his girlfriend. Why wouldn't she rejoice over that?

Patrick lifted his gaze from a pad of paper. His eyes locked onto hers, and his half-smile fell from his lips. "Kristine? What are you doing here?" He sounded frightened.

Kristine was puzzled. She stepped lightly toward him, saying, "Did you come here to meet me?" But why wasn't he at work? It didn't make sense.

Patrick stood and rolled his shoulders back. Kristine was suddenly aware that something was very off. His eyes were stony and unfriendly, as though they'd hardly met before. He felt like a stranger.

"I had my exit interview," Kristine said simply, her voice very soft.

Patrick palmed the back of his neck. Kristine had a sudden memory of being dumped by an ex-boyfriend, one she'd really thought had liked her. Suddenly, Richard's office door opened, and he stepped out, leering at Kristine with that horrible, familiar smile.

"Good afternoon, Kristine. I see you've met Patrick?" Richard extended a hand to shake his.

Kristine stuttered, confused. *What on earth was going on?*

"He's here to interview for your position," Richard continued. "He sent me a killer resumé, along with an assurance of his commitment to myself and my business. I couldn't ask for a better mindset here at the company. Don't you agree?"

Chapter Five

The light was overwhelming. Kim clamped her eyes shut again as her head throbbed with confusion. Something had happened. Something terrible. She could feel the truth of it in the pit of her stomach. *But what?*

Calm down. Breathe, Kim ordered herself. She'd been through enough in her life to know not to panic, as it always made everything worse. Whatever had happened, she would get through it. She had to.

But where was she? Her fingers were pressed against something scratchy. *Bedsheets, perhaps?* Clearly, she was lying down because she sensed that her legs were stretched out in front of her. But if she was in bed, then these bedsheets were not her own. She knew this because she'd treated herself to very expensive and luxurious sheets for Christmas. "I sleep in this bed alone," she'd told Jennifer, her daughter. "I might as well make it a lap of luxury."

Again, Kim attempted to open her eyes. She managed to hold them open just the slightest bit so that she could make out a small, well-lit room lined with large windows. Although everything was fuzzy, she thought she could make out a bouquet of flowers and a floating balloon on the far end of the room.

And then, there was the penetrating "beep, beep, beep" of a machine. Kim realized the beeping had been going since she'd woken up, but she'd only just registered it. She attempted to turn her head to find the source of the noise, but pain shot up and down her neck and back like rockets.

A soft groan came from her throat. She didn't fully recognize it as her own. It sounded more like an animal noise.

"Mom?" Jennifer's voice rang out from the corner of the room. In a flash, a figure hovered over Kim, one with jet-black hair and a very foggy face.

Kim blinked again, and the face shifted, presenting a sharper nose and those gorgeous sapphire eyes. This was her darling daughter, Jennifer. This was the beautiful baby she'd once birthed, who'd stuck around Bar Harbor and raised her children there. They'd even been blessed with Oliver, Kim's great-grandchild, about three years ago.

The worry that echoed back in Jennifer's eyes, along with her raggedy hairstyle and her red-tinged eyes, told Kim that whatever had happened had been serious.

"Mom, can you hear me?" Jennifer asked, her voice panicked.

Kim opened her lips wider, searching for words. Of course, she could hear Jennifer. But why, then, couldn't she speak? There was tremendous pressure against her throat. Was there something in her mouth?

Suddenly, Heather hustled up beside Jennifer, squeezed Kim's arm gently, and whispered, "It's okay, honey. You won't be able to speak. Not until they take out the breathing machine.

Breathing machine? Kim's panic spiked. It was clear she was in a hospital room and that she'd been in that hospital room long enough to require a breathing machine. How terrifying that her body hadn't known how to breathe on its own.

"I'll run and get the nurse," Heather said to Jennifer, as though Kim couldn't hear her. "You stay here."

Jennifer leaned forward and kissed her mother's arm and hand. Kim could barely feel her daughter's lips.

"It's okay, Momma. It's okay," Jennifer whispered.

Kim's thoughts spun with fear. How long had she been there? *What had happened?* She opened her eyes wider, and they jumped around the room so that she could see upwards of twenty flower bouquets, several more balloons, cards, and stuffed animals. Were they all for her?

Gosh, she'd never felt like more of a little old lady. At seventy, she'd thought of herself as a wild woman with at least fifty years left of a good life to live (this, she knew, was an exaggeration— but she liked to live in exaggeration, as she felt it kept her young).

"I don't know how much you remember," Jennifer continued. "You were snowmobiling back home from the Keating House on New Year's Day. You ran off the road and hit a tree. Since then, you've been in a coma."

Kim's heart thudded dully. *A coma?* She'd only ever seen comas on television or read about them in overly dramatic books. She didn't know it could actually happen to people in real life.

"Today is February 2nd, Mom," Jennifer said, her voice lifting. "I've been here every single day, praying to God that you would wake up. And here you are."

Jennifer sniffled and began to sob, overcome with fear and relief. More than anything, Kim wanted to reach across the bed and wrap her daughter in a hug. More than anything, she wanted to tell Jennifer that she would never leave her. This, Kim knew, was a lie. If anything, this accident had proven that Kim didn't have any control over what happened to her. *Life had its plans for you, regardless of what you wanted.*

* * *

Minutes later, Heather and two nurses entered the room. The two nurses were in their forties, and they were overjoyed with Kim's return to the world. Obviously, they'd spent a lot of time with Kim, hours that Kim would never remember. As she couldn't speak or lift herself up at all, Kim managed to wave her fingers at the women, hoping that they translated that as, "Thank you."

"She's a trooper," one of the nurses said to Jennifer, who continued to cry. "It'll be a long road to recovery, but she'll get there."

"If there's anyone who can, it's our Kim," the other nurse said.

Our Kim? Kim wanted to laugh aloud. She was nobody's "Kim." She wouldn't be treated like a child. Then again, she was even more helpless than her great-grandchild, Oliver. Even he could feed himself and walk around.

The doctor arrived and congratulated Kim on waking up. He adjusted his glasses and sat in a plastic chair beside her, assessing his clipboard.

"You're probably experiencing a number of very strange and painful sensations right now," he said matter-of-factly. "As you haven't used your muscles at all in a month, you will need rehabilitation to relearn how to walk."

Kim's eyes widened with fear. She'd assumed that the "inability to walk" thing would last a day, maybe three.

"Once we get the feeding tube out, you should be able to start eating solids within the week," the doctor continued. "It will be a painful transition, but a quick one, thankfully."

Kim blinked several times, telling herself not to cry. She'd awoken from a life-altering coma. She had to be patient with herself.

The doctor went on, telling her how much longer she would be in the hospital, that she would have to rent a wheelchair to get around her house, and that he would write her a prescription for pain, which she could pick up from the downstairs pharmacy. He then told her something that she already knew, which was: "You were very lucky. We don't always see patients come out of comas like this." He paused, tilted his head, then added, "There are a number of potential side-effects after head injuries of this kind. Don't be surprised if you're a bit confused over the next few months. Short-term memory might be difficult to hold onto. Also, there is a risk of seizures after an event like this."

"Seizures?" Jennifer gasped from the side of the room.

The doctor nodded. "But I believe you can make a full recovery, Kim. Let's work together to get you well again."

When the doctor left, a nurse arrived to remove Kim's breathing machine. Kim's lips relaxed together, and the pain in her throat and mouth subsided. Jennifer and Heather sat on either side of her, holding both of her hands.

"You won't be able to talk right away," the nurse informed her. "It's a process. But I know you'll be back to your old self in no time."

Kim dropped her gaze, terrified of words like "process" and "you were lucky." Most of all, she ached with guilt for having put her family through this pain. Why hadn't she given up on the snowmobile at fifty-five or sixty? Was she insane?

Kim was split. On the one hand, she wanted her daughter close, as she was terrified to be in the hospital alone. On the other, she hated that she couldn't speak to Jennifer or Heather, that she just lay between them like a very old, decrepit person. This wasn't like her.

Finally, Jennifer understood. When Heather got up to use

the bathroom down the hall, Jennifer whispered, "Listen, Mom. I know this is hard on you. I'll tell Heather to head home, and I'll read in the corner for a while. No pressure on either of us. Besides, the doctor says you need your sleep."

Kim's nostrils flared. She hoped it was enough to signal her thanks.

When Heather left, she squeezed Kim's hand gently and said, "I know you're dying to get out of there, come over to the Keating House, drink a glass of wine, and gossip the hours away with me. By summertime, all will be well again. I just know it."

In the silence of the late afternoon, Kim eyed her daughter in the corner, overwhelmed with love and gratefulness. There was no telling how many days on earth she had left. She would make the most of them when her body let her.

Chapter Six

T he wheels struck the airstrip at forty minutes past three. Outside, Maine snow spit from an ominous gray sky, and little yellow trucks whizzed around the airport, carting luggage to and from the airplanes. Kristine zipped her sweatshirt all the way to her chin, dropped her head back on the seat, and watched as Bella turned her phone back on after Airplane Mode. By the time the plane had stopped, Bella's thumbs had already crafted a very long and poetic text to Florian about how much she would miss him while they were away.

Kristine's stomach dropped. Since Kristine and Patrick's breakup, Bella and Florian had jumped into a relationship of their own. Kristine was happy for her sister— of course, she was. Then again, she wasn't so keen on seeing the new lovers' happiness as she limped from the kitchen to her bedroom and back again. She'd spent the weeks since the breakup nibbling on snacks, watching bad Netflix dating shows and crime dramas, and avoiding her phone like the plague. Most of her friends wanted to text and gossip about Patrick and how heinous he was. Kristine's heart wasn't in it. A part of her still loved him. Another part still loved the life she'd hoped they would share.

"This is going to be great." Bella lodged her phone in her pocket and jumped up to grab her backpack from the overhead compartment.

Kristine grumbled as Bella handed over her backpack. "If you say so."

Bella stuck out her tongue but didn't push it. Bella understood Kristine's tremendous heartache. Heck, Kristine had probably kept her twin sister up many nights with her crying.

The idea to come to Bar Harbor had been Bella's. She'd phrased it like this: "Gosh, I really need to get away from the city to focus on the rest of my paintings. I can't believe my art show is just a few weeks away! I'm freaking out! Would you go with me to Bar Harbor? You'd be doing me a favor."

In reality, Kristine knew Bella wanted to get Kristine out of the city, where their mother could take care of her. The breakup and the career derailment had torn her in two.

Heather and Luke waited for them in Luke's pickup truck. Heather dove from the truck and hugged them, her eyes overly large and blue when she caught Kristine's gaze. Yeah, yeah. Everyone was worried about her. It was embarrassing, to say the least.

Then again, Kristine was so grateful to be out of New York. She'd been on the verge of a nervous breakdown. During a job interview last week, she'd burst into tears. Then, she'd forced herself on a Tinder date, where she'd listened to the guy list all of his post-graduate accomplishments while she drank cocktail after cocktail.

Kristine and Bella loaded their suitcases in the bed of the truck, jumped into the back, and buckled their seatbelts. Traffic around the little airport was basically non-existent, and Luke got them safely to the highway in no time. A pang in the bottom of Kristine's stomach reminded her that the man in the front seat of the truck should have been her father, Max.

Luke was great. Fantastic, even. But he would never be her father.

"How is Aunt Kim doing?" Bella asked, leaning over her knees to talk to their mother.

Heather turned to scrunch her nose. "It's been a very traumatic week for her. She's finally back at home and talking a bit more. I think she's grateful to be out of the hospital, but she's certainly not back to her old self. Not by a long shot."

"A month is such a long time," Bella breathed.

"Yes. That's the problem. Her muscles have atrophied," Heather explained.

"I didn't know they could go so quickly," Kristine said.

Heather nodded. "Jennifer and I have tried our best to keep her spirit up. Somebody has to be around at all times."

"Have you thought about hiring a nurse?" Bella asked.

Heather shook her head. "We almost lost her." Her voice was sharp with emotion. "I don't want to put her in the care of anyone else. I don't want her to feel lonely for even a moment."

The Keating House and surrounding hills were covered with glistening snow. The parking lot outside the Keating Inn and Acadia Eatery was half-full, a surprise given the winter season. Heather explained that Abby and Hannah's photography business had been a boon for the marketing of the old place, bringing his travelers far and wide who were hungry for some "very cold, yet very beautiful New England adventures."

Kristine's heart lifted into her throat. A strange voice in the back of her mind told her this was home. She soon shoved that thought away, reminding herself the only "home" she had was the one she'd built for herself in the city. That was her future. This was just a blip.

Inside, Abby and Hannah sat at the kitchen table, editing photographs they'd recently taken of a young couple with a baby. Abby and Hannah greeted Kristine and Bella joyfully, jumping up to hug them.

"These are beautiful," Bella said, eyeing the photos on the computer screen. "But where is that darling baby of yours, Hannah?"

Hannah blushed. "We're taking a much-needed break from each other this afternoon. She kept me up all night last night."

"Oh no," Bella said, turning to open the fridge on the hunt for snacks.

"Don't let that sway you from having children of your own," Heather joked, her sapphire eyes glittering. Under her breath, she hissed, "Hannah, you're ruining my chances of becoming a grandmother one day!"

Hannah laughed. "Oh. I meant to say I'm always well slept! I feel fantastic!" She smiled.

"Nobody dotes on that little girl more than you," Abby teased.

"She's spoiled. That's actually the reason for all of my problems," Hannah agreed.

Heather stepped behind Bella, grabbed a large, covered platter from within the fridge, and announced, "I have a nice charcuterie board here. Who wants some?"

Heather, Kristine, and Bella gathered in the living room, collapsing on the cushioned couch, and prepared to feast on the greatest snack known to mankind: a wide variety of cheeses, crackers, grapes, hummus, and nuts. Heather rubbed Kristine's back and said, "Eat up, honey!" Maybe Bella had mentioned that Kristine's eating habits had been erratic. But could Kristine blame her sister for worrying about her? Slowly, she selected a cracker and a piece of cheese and crunched down.

"Note the lack of carrot sticks," Bella offered, her eyes flashing with the memory of Patrick and his judgemental ways.

"Bella," Heather warned.

"No. It's okay." Kristine scrunched her nose. "Now that I'm back home, I have a bit more context on the situation. I think."

"You have to be patient with yourself," Heather said. "You and Patrick were really serious. It's not every day you bring a guy home to meet us."

Heather stiffened. "I thought we were serious. I can't believe how wrong I was."

"We've all been wrong!" Heather reminded her. "Every woman I know has made a bad call when it comes to a man."

"Not you," Kristine pointed out. "You fell in love with Dad when you were really young. And after that, you met Luke."

Heather grimaced. "It didn't seem so easy at the time. I had my share of heartaches before your father."

Kristine wasn't sure she believed her. She locked eyes with Bella for a split second before returning her attention to the charcuterie board.

Bella wrapped her hand around Kristine's wrist. "I think instead of mourning, we should celebrate. You're dusting yourself off from that stupid job and that very mean man. Neither of those things were good for your psyche."

"Yes. But we also know you worked hard to get that job," Heather chimed in. "Nobody's saying you didn't deserve it."

"Come on. All he did was belittle you and make you get his coffee," Bella said. "It was basically like *The Devil Wears Prada*, without all the nice clothes."

For once, Kristine allowed herself to chuckle. "And a whole lot less of Meryl Streep."

"She's a gift to the world," Bella said.

Heather's laughter bubbled gently. "You two are hilarious."

Kristine rubbed her temples, her eyes to the corner, where a photograph of Bella, Kristine, Max, and Heather hung, a reminder of better days.

"I have no idea what I'm supposed to do next," Kristine

breathed, surprising herself with her honesty. "I had a perfect script set for the next ten years of my life. Now, all that has fallen apart."

Suddenly, Heather's phone buzzed on the small table next to the couch. Heather muttered, "I'm sorry, honey," and reached for it. "It's Jennifer. I have to take it."

Heather jumped up and stepped toward the foyer. "Hey, Jen. How is she?"

Kristine and Bella nibbled on crackers, listening to their mother's very brief conversation. Kristine alternated between feeling safe and very much like a fool. *What kind of woman fell for a guy like Patrick? Wasn't he so obviously lame?*

"Oh, yes. Of course. We can be there in twenty minutes!" Heather replied on the phone. "Don't worry at all."

Bella and Kristine turned back toward their mother as she re-entered the room.

"Where are we going?" Kristine asked.

"Jennifer's grandson has a bad fever," Heather explained, ruffling her long black hair. "She needs to take him to the hospital, which means we're needed at Kim's. Are you up for it?"

Chapter Seven

"You need to get him to the hospital. Don't worry about me." Kim's voice wavered strangely. Since she'd relearned how to speak, she didn't fully recognize the voice as her own.

Jennifer's cheeks were nearly as flushed as little Oliver's. His temperature had spiked to one hundred and four that afternoon, and with Oliver's mother working all afternoon and into the evening, Jennifer was the only one available to take him in.

"I just hate leaving you," Jennifer whispered, clearly at a loss.

"The girls are coming," Kim said, raising her hand slightly. "We'll have a ball together. Don't worry about us."

Jennifer scrunched her nose. Kim hated that Jennifer had committed so much time to Kim's wellness. It made her feel even more like a little old lady without control of her body. Then again, Kim literally couldn't do anything. She had a wheelchair, which she could maneuver around the house with the press of a button. Sometimes, pressing the button exhausted her finger and arm so much that, when headed to the kitchen, she had to pause in the center of the living room and wait for the moment of exhaustion to pass.

Needless to say, this was one of the most difficult times of her life. Oliver's illness and endless crying only exacerbated things.

"And you're sure it's okay to have all three of them here?" Jennifer scuttled around, collecting the diaper bag, a change of clothes for Oliver, plus snacks for the both of them. "That's a pretty full house."

Kim nodded, wincing slightly at the pain along her neck. "Heather, Kristine, and Bella are family."

"They're new family," Jennifer pointed out distractedly. "I've told you before. You don't have to think of Heather like a daughter just because your sister treated her so terribly."

Kim bristled, surprised at her daughter's unkindness. Jennifer winced, as well.

"I'm sorry. I really am," Jennifer said. "I'm just stressed."

Suddenly, there was a knock at the door. Jennifer breezed through the foyer to open it. Heather's voice came through, a welcoming sound in the midst of Oliver's weeping.

"Oh, poor baby," Heather said. "You go ahead, Jennifer. We'll take care of everything."

Kristine and Bella stepped through the foyer and into the living room, where Kim was propped up in her wheelchair. The women were twenty-three and spectacularly gorgeous, with the same genetic beauty that Kim, Melanie, Heather, and Jennifer all had enjoyed. Their faces smiled, but their eyes were heavy with confusion and pity. Kim resented this, although she knew there was nothing to be done about it. She was a woman of seventy in a wheelchair. Pity was coming for her, whether she wanted it or not.

"Hi, Aunt Kim!" Bella spoke first. She lifted a bag of groceries and said, "I hope you're hungry in a bit. We were thinking of eggplant parmesan for dinner."

Kristine sat on the couch next to Kim. Up close, her eyes were strangely shadowed and lacked their familiar youthfulness. The last time Kim had seen her, she'd had that terrible businessman boyfriend who'd seen it his duty to belittle the rest of the family. Had he hurt her in some way? It seemed like something he would do.

"Eggplant Parmesan sounds delightful," Kim croaked.

Heather breezed into the living room, her smile a light in the darkness. "Aunt Kim. Hi." She dropped down to kiss her on the cheek. "Poor little Oliver! I've never seen him so sick." She adjusted on the couch next to Kristine, then said, "I'm so glad to have my girls home with me today. We thought we'd have a girls' night all together." She searched through another grocery bag and removed two bottles of wine. "I know you shouldn't drink alcohol so soon after your brain injury. But at the store, they had a special on non-alcoholic wine. What do you think about that?"

Kim snorted. "Isn't that just juice?"

Both Bella and Kristine cackled.

Heather tilted her head to-and-fro. She was trying to keep everything upbeat. Bless her. Kim wasn't sure she could follow her lead.

"I think it's a little more decadent than juice," Heather insisted.

"All right." Kim rolled her eyes playfully. "I have missed my evening glasses of wine. I might as well give it a shot."

In the kitchen, Heather and Bella set to work on cooking the eggplant parmesan while Kristine sat at the kitchen table. Kim wheeled her chair up to the table as well and heaved a sigh of exhaustion. Heather snapped on the radio, which played Bruce Springsteen's "Dancing in the Dark," which had always been one of Kim's favorite songs.

"Goodness. This song takes me back," Kim said. She eyed

her legs, which were now useless to her. There was no dancing in her immediate future. That was clear.

"He was such a hunk," Bella said, her knife flashing through an onion.

"Was? He still is," Heather corrected.

Kristine laughed gently, her eyes on the ground. Heather soon uncorked both the alcoholic and non-alcoholic bottles of wine and poured the four of them glasses. Kim used all her strength to lift her glass in the air to "cheers" the other girls. Their eyes remained on her as she sipped it. The oaky, berry "wine" coated her tongue, reminding her of beautiful wine nights with friends and lovers gone-by.

"It's not that bad," Kim said with a smile.

"I'll take it as a win." Heather turned back to the skillet, where she'd begun to stir up a very garlicky tomato sauce. The air was heavy with delicious smells.

It took a long time to make the eggplant parmesan. To Kim's surprise, the time passed beautifully, with the radio kicking out all the hits from the eighties (her favorite era of music) and Bella and Heather gossiping easily about people in the city and people in Bar Harbor. Kristine was frequently very quiet, but even she came forward with the occasional story about someone she and Bella hung out with in New York.

It was only over dinner that Kim got the story of what had happened between Kristine and that terrible ex-boyfriend of hers.

Kim's fork was lifted, her jaw open with shock. "Are you kidding me? He went after the job you'd just left. And he didn't bother to mention it?"

Kristine rolled her eyes sadly. "He said I would find some-thing else— that I was too talented to stay in that position anyway. Oh, but he was nothing but a liar. I'd seen him lie to so many people before me. Why did I think he wouldn't lie to me, too?"

"That's the thing about guys," Kim offered. "Some of them, anyway."

"What, exactly?" Kristine asked.

"Once they figure out how to lie to you, they do it over and over again. It's like they can't help it," Kim said.

Kristine scrunched her nose. "They can't all be liars."

"They're not," Heather interjected, her sapphire eyes flashing.

Kim laughed, for a moment forgetting the pain that was so heavy in her body. "Yes. Then again, you seem to have a talent for finding some of the most perfect men in the world. What's your secret?"

"That's what I said!" Kristine cried.

"Aunt Kim. Tell us about your ex-husband!" Bella chimed in eagerly.

"Goodness." Kim swallowed a generous bite of cheese, eggplant, and tomato sauce. It seemed to warm her from the inside. "My ex-husband was a real piece of work. I can tell you that. We met in Portland at a dance club that has long since closed its doors forever."

"A dance club. Wow. It's like a movie," Bella breathed.

"He was just about as handsome as they made them back then," Kim said, suddenly overwhelmed with nostalgia. "He came over to me and asked me to dance. You know what I said?"

"No! What?" Kristine asked.

"I said no." Kim cackled. "I just hated how arrogant he looked, coming over to me like he owned the place and everyone in it."

Bella, Heather, and Kristine laughed good-naturedly. Probably, they all thought of her as a little old lady, her stories so deep in the past that they didn't matter at all. Still, all Kim had now were those memories.

"He fought for me after that," Kim continued. "It was some

kind of warrior instinct. He figured out where I lived, and he left me little notes and flowers. My roommate called him my stalker. Still, I said no to him until, one night, I caught his band performing at a little bar. He could sing like nothing else. My heart completely cracked open for him. He saw me in the crowd, stopped the performance, and walked right up to me. I'll never forget what he said."

"What was it?" Bella, Heather, and Kristine leaned over the table, captivated.

"He said, 'I've already moved on. I've met someone new.'" Kim laughed at the memory, still remembering the urgency and anger in his eyes. "I knew, of course, that whatever new relationship he had didn't matter much. By the end of the week, we'd found a way to spend nearly every waking moment together. And by the end of the year, we were married."

"That's so romantic," Kristine breathed.

"Yes. It was." Kim shook her head. "It hardly seems like real life. Certainly not like my life."

"Oh, come on. You're a knock-out," Bella said.

Kim placed her fork to the side of the plate with a clack. She didn't feel like a knockout just then, especially being wheelchair-bound and with her thoughts mushy from the medication. She felt like nothing good would ever happen to her again.

Heather insisted that Kim relax in the living room while she and Bella washed the dishes. Kim agreed, sipping the silly non-alcoholic wine as Kristine flicked through television channels. They eventually landed on *Four Weddings and a Funeral*, a classic romcom from the nineties.

"Hugh Grant was so charming," Kristine said with a sad smile. "But should we ever trust the charming ones?"

"My husband was not a bad husband for a very long time," Kim tried, hoping to impart some level of hope to the poor girl. "In fact, when we did divorce, we did so out of mutual respect rather than anger at one another. Everything was very fluid. We didn't even hire separate lawyers."

Kristine grimaced. Probably, the subject of divorce was a very grim one to such a young woman. She wanted everything to go well for her, without pain and heartache. This was simply impossible.

"You know Patrick is miserable," Kim spoke through the silence. "His entire identity is tied up in this stupid job. What's more, all his friends know you got the job first. People are talking behind his back, and he knows it."

"I don't know. He has too much money to ever care what people think of him," Kristine said.

"People with money worry even more about what people think of them," Kim returned. "They're not like you and I. They haven't fallen on hard times before. A bit of gossip is the worst of their worries."

Kristine wrinkled her nose. She then locked eyes with Kim and said, "I'm sorry to blabber on about guys. So much has happened to you lately. I can't even imagine."

Kim waved her hand slowly, suddenly overwhelmed with fatigue. "All I want is to forget. Thank you for helping me to do that, at least for a little while."

"Stupid gossip about boys does the trick?"

"It's the only thing that does," Kim told her.

On the television screen, Hugh Grant wore his crooked grin, attempting to woo a beautiful American in a very large hat. Kim's heart beat slowly, and she coated her tongue with the non-alcoholic wine again. Around her, the house was warm, filled with the sounds of clunking dishes and Heather and Bella's chirping gossip. For a moment, she felt at peace.

Chapter Eight

A scream came from the back hallway of the Keating House. Kristine bolted from the reading nook and into Bella's makeshift art studio, where Bella gaped at her painting, her paintbrush pointed toward the sky.

"What?" Kristine demanded.

Bella turned, her face white with shock. "I made a huge mistake."

Kristine eyed the painting, which was abstract and bizarre. It made her feel as though the world was crooked. Kristine was no artist, of course, but to her, there was no mistake to be seen.

"I lost focus," Bella admitted, turning back toward her painting. "Come on, Bella. Get it together."

"Be easier on yourself, Bell," Kristine said softly. "Everything you do is gorgeous."

Bella made a soft sound in the back of her throat. She appreciated the compliment, but she obviously wasn't sure she believed Kristine. That was all right, for now.

Kristine stepped back into the hallway, leaving her sister to her devices. With only a few weeks left till the gallery show,

Bella spent eight-hour days at her canvas, only appearing in the kitchen for cups of coffee and snacks. Caught in the chaos of her artistic mind, she'd hardly brushed her hair in days. Privately, Heather and Kristine called her "Van Gogh." "How's Van Gogh doing in there?" Of course, they loved her and were so proud of her success. Still, it was funny to witness the lengths of her artistic insanity.

Heather was off at Aunt Kim's for the day, and the rest of the Keating-Harvey clan was in various pockets of their everyday lives. Kristine knew if she stepped into the Keating Inn, she would probably find Luke and Nicole at the Eatery and maybe even Abby at the front desk. Downtown, she would find cousin Brittany at the antique shop and Hannah safe at home with her baby. At the new house, Aunt Casey was hard at work on architectural designs for a new and very particular client, which had made her difficult to be around.

Kristine had never felt more useless.

She dressed warmly and stepped into the forty-degree day, which was much warmer than a typical day in February in Bar Harbor. The air was bearable rather than sharply cold. With her hands in her pockets, she walked toward downtown Bar Harbor, focusing on her breathing and the glittering light across Frenchman Bay. This truly was a spectacular place in the world, one that she was lucky to call her own. She had to find a way to truly appreciate it.

When Kristine reached downtown, she stopped at a coffee shop to order a cappuccino. The coffeeshop was quaint, with child-made art adorning the walls. It had none of the "trendy vibes" of a typical Brooklyn coffeeshop, which was a relief just then. She sat at a corner table, sipped her cappuccino, and looked at Instagram, telling herself she would read an article soon.

Instead, she found herself clicking on Patrick's profile.

She hadn't allowed herself to look at it in over a week. Now, she found herself staring at his perfectly cultivated page, where he'd posted photos of himself at high-end corporate events. In some of the photos, he stood next to men Kristine had met through Richard— men who'd hardly glanced her way or taken stock of her ideas.

They took Patrick seriously. So seriously that they'd invited him to these exclusive events, peppered him with scotch cocktails, and laughed with him into the night. Patrick was a "chosen one," just as much as Kristine was not. Her cheeks burned with self-hatred.

Kristine finished her cappuccino and returned to Main Street, where a soft snow had begun to fall. Her head cloudy, she paused several times to peer into shop windows, where shop owners had arranged beautiful displays of flowers, fake cakes, and children's toys. There on Main Street, Kristine felt totally alone, her college degree a waste of her time and effort. Why had she done all those all-nighters? Why had she thought she was so special? That she had to make it?

Two blocks later, Kristine paused outside a local cookie and candy shop called Sweet Thing. Kristine had had their homemade chocolates before, and they were sinfully decadent. The part of her that felt bad for herself demanded she enter, purchase a cookie, and eat it in one go. The bell jingled as she pressed through the door, surprising her. It was rare that she gave into her impulses, perhaps because Patrick and the rest of the city had trained her to "watch her figure."

"Good afternoon." A woman of about fifty stepped behind the counter. "Can I help you?"

Kristine studied the various flavors of cookies: chocolate chip, peanut butter, oatmeal raisin, and double chocolate. The cookies were four inches in diameter, which was a mountain of food.

Under the display case of cookies, a sign fluttered in the soft wind from the heater.

HELP WANTED - INQUIRE AT THE REGISTER

Kristine's lips parted with surprise. A job? Was that something she wanted? It would certainly fill her days up and give her something to think about besides her failures.

"I'll take a peanut butter cookie and..." She stalled, unsure of what she wanted. "And an application?"

* * *

After Bella finished painting later that afternoon, Kristine handed her a cookie and said, "I got a job."

Bella arched her eyebrow, which was peppered with yellow paint. She took a large bite of her oatmeal raisin cookie and said, "Like something online?"

"No." Kristine nodded toward the cookie. "Sweet Thing needed help. Twenty hours a week."

Bella's jaw dropped. "What are you talking about? You got hired at that tiny cookie store downtown?"

Kristine nodded. "I'm not too good to work at a candy store."

Bella stuttered. "Nobody is saying you're too good for that. It's just that, well." She paused to consider what she wanted to say. "You need to be thinking about what's next for you. Right? That's what this trip to Bar Harbor is all about?"

"I thought our trip was all about your paintings," Kristine shot back.

"Yes. Of course." Bella grimaced. "But also, you've just gone through something pretty traumatic. I don't know if working at a candy shop will solve that?"

"I just hate sitting around here all day, thinking about everything I've done wrong," Kristine said. "It makes me feel insane."

Bella considered this. "Did you tell her you have a college degree and everything?"

"She said she was expecting someone a bit younger," Kristine said with a laugh. "But I told her I knew my way around a cash register, and she hired me on the spot."

Heather entered the kitchen after that, bringing in a chill that followed her from outside. "Cookies! Yum!" She removed her coat and collapsed at the table, taking a chocolate chip from Kristine's collection.

"Yes. Kristine is starting a brand-new career. She's working minimum wage at the cookie store," Bella announced.

Heather eyed Kristine, the color fading from her cheeks. Kristine gave her mother a look of confidence. *Wasn't Kristine the only one who had any say in what Kristine did?*

"Well." Heather considered this for a long moment, her cookie lifted. "I hope that means we'll feast on cookies all winter long."

"No doubt about it," Kristine said. "We'll be well-supplied. You have my word."

Chapter Nine

The Bar Harbor Winter Festival was held every year in early to mid-February. It was a time to celebrate all things "cold weather," like ice skating competitions, snowmobile races, hot apple cider (often with a bit of rum), hot chili, and plenty of communion. Bar Harbor residents used the weekend as a way to pause between New Year's and springtime, to breathe and take in the splendor of their snow-capped surroundings. It was a necessary interlude, a time only for them — the Maine locals who knew how to handle winter weather and how to enjoy it.

Kim had always looked forward to the Bar Harbor Winter Festival. In her childhood, she and Melanie had started the day early with the children's snowman-building competition, followed by a feast of stews, hot dogs, apple cider, and plenty of chocolate. As she'd gotten older, she'd found new ways of celebrating. For three years running, she'd won the female snowmobile race, and the medals currently lined her fireplace, proof of what a stellar rider she'd once been. Several years, she'd been allowed to race with the men, and she'd been a worthy contender, frequently coming close to the top three. Her husband had been both very proud and very resentful of this, never really sure what to do with his spitfire wife.

But this year was different than the other years. Kim was wheelchair-bound and largely incapable of anything but talking and eating by herself. She spent her days at the window, gazing out at Frenchman Bay and daydreaming about winters gone by. She'd never been afraid of the frigid winter and had always viewed it as a time of rest, of rebirth— that, and coziness with the ones she loved most. It seemed a shame she couldn't fully enjoy it. Maybe she never would again.

"You love the Winter Festival. Everyone would wonder where you were," Jennifer pleaded the morning of the festival, her eyes hungry to make everything all right again.

"Darling, everyone probably thinks I'm dead!" Kim returned, rubbing her temples.

"They do not. Everyone asks about you," Jennifer shot back. "They want you there, eating chili, cheering on the ice skaters, and gossiping with the rest of us."

Eventually, Kim found herself agreeing, although she had a hunch she would regret it. It took all of Jennifer's strength to get Kim into the back of her car, where Kim slowly fastened the seatbelt, having to concentrate with all her might. Once Jennifer got in the front seat, she turned and smiled at her mother, but her eyes told a different story: she regretted having asked.

With the use of Kim's handicapped sticker, they were able to park right downtown.

"Luxury parking!" Jennifer said brightly as she shut off the engine.

"Welcome to old age," Kim grunted. She'd never had to use that sticker before.

Jennifer eyed her. "Let's get something to eat. I'm starving."

Once Kim was back in her wheelchair and bundled up, she allowed herself to take in the beauty of another Winter Festival. Stalls lined the downtown streets, selling hot apple cider and pretzels and other foods that promised to stick to your bones. Bar Harbor residents who Kim had known her entire life passed by, stopping to smile at Kim (with a bit of pity, of course) and tell her how good it was to see her.

Still, Kim couldn't help it. Her smile widened with each conversation. Turns out she'd missed human interaction after all. *Who would have guessed?*

Kim and Jennifer purchased hot apple ciders and chili and sat in front of the ice-skating competition at a downtown outdoor rink that had been built just for the occasion. Bar Harbor treated its ice skating competitions like the Olympics, save for the fact that everyone was just an amateur. Yes, several young women were very good, wearing attractive costumes and kicking up into beautiful spins. Several other competitors were middle-aged men, many of them the fathers of these same ice skating teenagers, in ridiculous costumes, hoping to get a good laugh. Of course, Bar Harbor was a place for laughter— and there was even a "Best Comedy Routine" award.

"I think he's hilarious," Jennifer said, doubling over as a middle-aged dad danced around in a Flintstones costume and whacked a large stick on the ice like a caveman.

On the sidelines, his daughter alternated between shame and laughter. At the end of his show, she howled and clapped her hands, which made her father glow with happiness.

"Is that Aunt Kim?" A voice rang out to her left.

Kim turned quickly to find Heather, Bella, Nicole, Casey, and Abby walking toward her, each with hot apple cider or hot cocoa in their gloved hands.

"Jennifer dragged me outside," Kim joked.

"I did not," Jennifer shot back. "How are you ladies finding the festival?"

"It's just a dream," Heather said, tilting her head. "We've already eaten our weight in food."

"Then you're not quite done yet," Kim said.

"That's a woman after my own heart." Bella snapped her fingers as everyone laughed.

"Did you see that last performance?" Casey asked. "He killed it out there."

"Mom performed in the ice-skating competition a few years ago," Jennifer explained, eyeing Kim. "She wore a Cruella de Ville outfit and totally destroyed the competition."

"That isn't true," Kim quipped. "I did win 'Best Costume,' though."

"Well deserved!" Heather said.

"And where is the third triplet?" Kim asked, eyeing Bella and Heather. "There's normally one more of you."

"She had to work this afternoon, I'm afraid," Heather said, her eyes shadowed.

"She took a job at the cookie shop down the road," Bella explained, wrinkling her nose. "We wish she was out here with us. She keeps texting me about how bored she is. I mean, I told her not to work a minimum-wage job!"

"Sometimes, it's good to have something to do," Jennifer tried.

"Sure." Bella seemed unconvinced.

"Oh no. Not that cookie shop?" Kim was worried. She'd had a few run-ins with the woman who owned the place and wasn't exactly her biggest fan.

"Why? What's wrong?" Heather could sense Kim's unease.

"Oh, nothing. Nothing. Why don't we go over there and say hello?" Kim suggested. "We've seen enough ice skaters for one day, I think. And I have a hunch one apple cider with rum won't kill me."

"Mom..." Jennifer warned.

"All right. All right." Kim waved her hand. "I'll stick to sober living for now. I heard it does wonder for the skin, anyway."

Jennifer wheeled Kim alongside Heather while Bella, Casey, Nicole, and Abby brought up the rear. Heather talked about the plot of her novel, which she was struggling with, and Kim relished it. It wasn't so common for Heather to reveal her creative process.

"You've got such a creative mind, Heather," Kim said softly. "I wish I could steal a bit of it. I know creativity is the first step toward optimism."

Heather's smile faltered. "I can imagine it's difficult to feel optimistic during this time, Aunt Kim. Know that we'll be there for you every step of the way. Even on the days when you feel especially grim."

Kim's eyes watered, threatening to spill tears.

"There she is!" Bella waved into the candy and cookie shop, Sweet Thing, where a very bored-looking Kristine manned the counter in a silly-looking pink apron and a pink hat to match. "Oh, look at her. I have to take a picture." Bella lifted her phone and snapped several photos, many of which featured Kristine waving her hand in protest.

A moment later, Kristine stormed out of the candy store, her smile angry. "Stop that, Bella!"

"You're going to want these later!" Bella returned.

Kristine laughed and quickly removed her hat, clearly embarrassed. "Hi, Aunt Kim! Gosh, it's good to see you."

Kim's heart swelled with love for the young and very lost girl. "I see you've found a new career."

Kristine shook her head. "Nothing like that. Just a way to pass the time and earn a bit of cash."

"It's responsible," Jennifer affirmed. To this, Bella cast her a dark look.

"We're so dead today," Kristine explained. "Everyone's

eating from the stalls at the festival. I asked my boss if I could lock up, but she said no."

"That's terrible," Heather said. "You're out in, what, two hours?"

"Three." Kristine scuffed her foot through the snow.

Because nobody was in the cookie shop, Kristine stood out on the street with them for a long while, chatting and gossiping about the goings-on at the festival. Bella updated her on everything she'd seen so far, which included a man dressed as Mickey Mouse parading through the street.

"Oh, that was the mayor," Kim said. "He does that every year."

"No kidding!" Bella and Kristine said in unison.

"This place is a fairy tale," Bella said.

"Oh, and the chili competition!" Heather continued. "Bella and I ate three bowls of chili. I thought I was going to get sick."

"But then, you suggested that we eat those cupcakes with buttercream frosting," Bella reminded her.

"Hey," Kim chimed in. "The Winter Festival comes but once a year. You have to live in the moment!"

Suddenly, a terrible shriek filled the air. Everyone turned back toward the candy shop, where four boys in thick winter hats and balaclavas stormed out, each with plastic bags filled with cookies and candy.

"Oh my gosh! They're stealing from you!" Nicole cried.

Kristine burst to life. "Hey! Get back here!" She scampered after them, her face stricken. Unfortunately, there was no chasing them down. These young boys took high school gym and were in better shape than all of them combined. They'd already ran around the corner by the time Kristine had made it a single block.

"Oh. No!" Heather whispered.

Kristine limped back to her crew, her eyes glittering with surprise. She then sputtered and entered the still-open door of the candy shop to assess the damage. Bella ran after her, followed by Jennifer, pushing Kim, Heather, Casey, Nicole, and Abby.

The boys had ransacked the place. They'd torn all the cookies from the display case, filled bags with candy, and even stolen the containers of whipped cream that normally sat on the counter.

Kristine breathed too quickly. "I don't know what to do. I don't know what to do."

"Honey. It's just candy," Heather reminded her. "You weren't in charge of a jewelry store."

"Yeah, but still. I was in charge." Kristine looked on the brink of collapse. She leafed through her pocket and found her phone, which she placed against her ear to call her boss. A few seconds later, her family listened in on her side of the phone call, which couldn't have gone worse.

"Hi. Um. Something happened here at the shop. We've been robbed. No, not the cash register. But all the cookies, most of the candy, and loads of other stuff." Kristine's lower lip bounced.

When Kristine finally hung up the phone, she collapsed against the counter and stared at the ground. "She fired me. She wants me to leave my apron behind and lock up."

"Fired you?" Bella looked livid.

Kristine shrugged. "I understand. I totally messed up."

"Oh, come on. I'll echo your mother. It's only candy." Kim rolled her eyes.

But Kristine was broken. This, on top of her breakup and the loss of her "big city" job, seemed to be too much. She asked that everyone leave so she could lock up the place. A few minutes later, she appeared on the sidewalk, a broken woman without a pink apron.

"Let's get you a hot apple cider with rum," Bella said, her arm around Kristine's shoulders.

"I think I need it," Kristine said.

As they headed back toward the festival, Kim had an idea. Without running it past her daughter first, she said, "Hey. Kristine. Can I talk to you for a sec?"

Kristine turned to face Kim in her wheelchair. "Of course. What's up?"

Jennifer stopped the chair so they could speak. Kim could feel Jennifer's confusion.

"As you know, I have a bit of an issue with, well, doing basically everything," Kim said. "Walking. Cooking. Cleaning. Everything."

Kristine stuttered. "It's only temporary."

"Yes. Just like your situation here in Bar Harbor is only temporary. Why don't you come by my house and give me a hand? It would give Jennifer and Heather a break. Plus, I could pay you."

Kristine wrinkled her nose. "I don't want to be a charity case."

To this, Kim just laughed. "I feel the same about myself. Why don't we help each other?"

Chapter Ten

That night, as Bella relaxed in the living room with a glass of wine and flicked through television channels, Kristine set to work on the couch. A quick Google search told her a great deal about caring for immobile people, including tips to avoid making them feel inferior. *"It's important to remember: the people you care for still demand dignity and respect, despite their inability to get around as well. How would you feel in this situation? How would you like to be treated?"*

Kristine groaned and shoved her computer aside.

"What's wrong?" Bella turned from a home improvement show and gave Kristine a quizzical look.

"I don't know if I can do this," Kristine admitted. "Kim is recovering from a major health scare. I'm a washed-up business student who can't even hold down a job at a candy store."

"First of all, you wouldn't have lasted more than two weeks at that candy store without going insane," Bella said. "Secondly, from what I can tell, Kim is pretty easy-going about everything.

Mom and Jennifer cook her food and keep her company. That's about it."

"Yeah, but the internet says that coma patients are at a higher risk of complications," Kristine explained, her voice high-pitched and fearful. "What if something happens while I'm there?"

"That is scary. I know." Bella pondered for a moment. On-screen, the home improvement host tore through a wall with a sledgehammer. "But listen, if anything happens, you call the ambulance, just like Mom would," Bella finished.

Kristine understood what her sister meant. If something happened, it didn't matter if Kristine, Heather, Jennifer, or the Pope was there. As long as someone was around to call 9-1-1, that was all that mattered.

"Did you ever think about going into the medical field?" Kristine asked thoughtfully.

Bella scrunched her nose. "I'm terrified of blood."

"Right." Kristine laughed, overwhelmed with memories. "Remember when I skinned my knee on that bike ride? I barely felt anything, but blood gushed down my leg until Dad found a band-aide in his bag."

"Yeah, yeah. I screamed the entire time. I know." Bella smiled sadly. "You were always braver than I was. Now, I'm just a painter, so I can hide away in my room and work while you run off and conquer the world."

"I don't feel anywhere close to conquering it right now."

Bella shrugged. "You've been on top before. You will again."

Kristine's heart darkened. Why did everyone believe in her so much, even after so many previous failures? Maybe she wasn't cut out for the real world.

There was a knock at the door, followed by the friendly ding of the doorbell. As Heather was with Luke, Nicole was with Evan, and Abby was out for the night, the twins were the only ones home. Kristine leaped from the couch as Bella said, "Oh, thanks. I was going to get that."

"You didn't move a muscle," Kristine quipped.

"Yeah. But I thought about it," Bella shot back.

A man in his mid-twenties stood on the front porch. He wore a very thick navy coat and a wool hat, and dark curls spilled around his face and over his cheeks. His eyes were blue, yet terribly serious, and his lips did not smile, which was a rarity when people stopped by your house in Bar Harbor.

"Hello?" Kristine rubbed one of her feet against her ankle.

"Hi." The man lifted several brown paper bags from the porch floor and shrugged. "You're Kristine, right? And you were working at Sweet Thing this afternoon?"

Kristine tilted her head. This was very curious. "I was."

The guy tilted the brown paper bags so that Kristine could see inside. They held piles and piles of cookies and candies— maybe not everything that had been stolen, but very nearly. Kristine lifted her eyes to his, wincing.

Before she could ask any questions, he explained, "My teenage brother and his friends are infamous around town for performing little acts of, erm, robbery. I found them digging through their new 'finds' this evening. Most of the candy wrappings have logos for Sweet Thing, and I put two and two together."

Kristine arched her brow. "You decided to return them? To me?"

The guy shrugged, at a loss. "If I took them directly to the owner, she would figure out the connection and have my brother arrested. Seriously. She's that cruel."

"Wow. Arrested over candy," Kristine breathed. *Was this small-town drama at its finest?*

"But I couldn't exactly let them keep it," he continued. "So here I am, hoping you could pass it over to your boss? Maybe you could say you found it on the porch or something?"

Kristine laughed, suddenly at-ease. The guy was adorably embarrassed about his brother and the case of the stolen candy.

"Why don't you come in for a glass of wine or a cup of cocoa?"

The guy was taken aback. "Oh, I don't want to put you out."

"Seriously. You'd be saving me." Kristine eyed her computer, where she could make out the words: *"Top Ten Things to Remember When Caring for Someone After the Hospital."*

The guy entered the foyer, still carrying the bags of candy and cookies. He eyed Bella, who jumped up to get a better look at him.

"What do you have there?" Bella asked, eyeing the bags.

"This is, um." Kristine locked eyes with him again, realizing she didn't know his name.

"Carter. Carter Bilson." He waved and tried to smile but seemed too exhausted. "My little brother, TJ, stole from Kristine today."

Kristine's stomach twisted with excitement. How had he known her name? *Did things like that just get around small towns? Goodness. Wasn't this different than New York City living?*

"Are you here to make amends for what your brother has done?" Bella joked, stepping around to inspect the candy. She then dropped down and selected a very large oatmeal cookie with dried raspberries and white chocolate chips.

Carter eyed Kristine curiously. To this, Kristine laughed and said, "I was fired from the candy store already. To tell you the truth, I don't care what happens to any of this. I certainly won't be taking it back to that horrible woman. We might as well have a treat or two."

Kristine heated water for cocoa in the kitchen as Carter removed his winter coat and hat. Beneath, he was a sturdy-looking man with capable muscles, a flat stomach, and a smile that peeked out ever-so-slowly. Bella joined them in the kitchen for a while, sipping wine and asking Carter questions about the robbery.

"What else have they taken around town?"

Carter palmed his neck. "I shouldn't just blab that stuff around."

"I don't usually live here!" Bella said. "Your secret is safe with me."

"Well." Carter winced. "A few weeks ago, I'm pretty sure they stole seven very expensive steaks from a restaurant that belongs to Evan Snow. But I can't prove it."

Bella and Heather locked eyes and shared a secret laugh. It was better not to tell Carter that Evan was essentially their uncle.

"I heard Evan Snow isn't as mean as he used to be," Bella said.

"Sure. But I don't think he'd take too kindly about losing seven steaks worth eighty dollars each," Carter said. He rubbed his temples and added, "I've been TJ's guardian since he was twelve when our mother died. I feel part-father, part-brother, and I don't really know how to manage either. On top of that, I work strange hours, and I don't always have a good grip on where he is."

"That sounds really hard," Kristine breathed, passing him a cup of cocoa.

Bella nodded, a shadow passing over her face. She then took a delicate step back toward the living room, her eyes flashing. Kristine sensed what Bella wanted to do. She wanted to give Kristine time alone with Carter. Although this embarrassed Kristine to no end, she was oddly grateful for Bella's "twin understanding." It had been quite a while since she'd felt beautiful in a man's eyes— especially a man as handsome as Carter.

More than anything, Carter seemed to really need a friend.

Kristine sat across the kitchen table from Carter and blew the steam from the top of her hot cocoa.

"I got so angry when I found the candy and cookies today," Carter said under his breath. "I wanted to scream at him, to ask him what he thought I was working so hard for. Every day, I wake up, make breakfast, make sure he has his school books with him, take him to school, and worry about his future every single hour until I see him at night. I didn't get to go to college because I had to be around for him. And that's okay. But I really need him to take his life more seriously, if only because I haven't really been able to have one." Carter groaned and dropped his chin. "I know that isn't fair, either. TJ didn't choose any of this. He didn't want our mother to die."

Kristine sipped her hot cocoa, at a loss. From what Carter told her, he and TJ lived a much more difficult life than she did. Yes, "boo hoo,"— she was taking time off from the corporate world, and she'd gotten dumped. But then again, she didn't have to care for a sibling like TJ. She didn't have to kill herself, working to make ends meet.

When Kristine had dated Patrick, she'd been very aware of Patrick's wealth at all times. Besides his clothing, even his skin exuded wealth, fitness, and good health. With Carter, Kristine was very aware of the enormous and very warm house around her, the beautiful forest on the far end of the property, and the prosperity of the Keating Inn and Acadia Eatery. There was no struggling there. There was always enough food to go around.

"You should take some of these cookies and candies back with you," Kristine said as Carter prepared to leave a little while later. "Really."

But Carter was adamant. "I have to show TJ that stealing isn't going to be rewarded. We all have to live in the same society. He has to get on board with that."

Kristine nodded sadly. Life was unfair; it was always a

question of what family you were born into and what luck you had along the way.

"Thanks again, Carter," Kristine murmured as Carter stepped from the threshold and into the swirling snow of the evening. "And to me, it sounds like your brother is lucky to have you."

Carter sighed and waved a hand. There were heavy circles beneath his eyes, not from age, but from exhaustion. Kristine watched him as he trudged through the snow, laced his leg over his snowmobile, and then sped out of sight.

"Wow!" Bella shrieked from the couch, her eyes enormous.

Kristine collapsed next to her, overwhelmed. "That was unexpected."

"You're telling me. I didn't know they made guys who look like that in Bar Harbor," Bella teased.

"He seems so lonely," Kristine breathed. "Like he doesn't have anyone to talk to."

"He has you," Bella joked.

Kristine rolled her eyes, took Bella's glass of wine from her hand, and sipped. Memory of the way Carter's eyes had burned with fear, sorrow, and loss would haunt her for the rest of the night.

"I have a feeling you'll be seeing Mr. Carter Bilson again soon," Bella said mischievously. "Mark my words. I'm never wrong."

Chapter Eleven

Jennifer wasn't pleased about the Kristine arrangement. She hovered in the foyer, watching the driveway like a hawk, while Kim waited in the living room.

"She's late," Jennifer said ominously.

"She's one minute late," Kim shot back. "When you were twenty-three, you would have called right now to tell me you still needed thirty minutes to get ready."

Jennifer turned, her face stony. "Exactly my point! Twenty-three-year-olds are not responsible. I swear, the minute things go sour here, you'd better call me. I can come back right away."

Kim wheeled herself toward the foyer, recognizing there was more strength in her arms than there'd been a few days before. Progress.

"Jen, all you've done since I got out of the hospital is run around here, worrying yourself to death," Kim said. "Frankly, it's freaking me out."

Jennifer smiled slightly and palmed the back of her neck. Before she could go on, Kim added, "We need to figure out a way for you to get back to your life. Since the accident, I know that you've spent more time at the hospital and here with me than anywhere else."

Jennifer stuttered. "There's nowhere else I'd rather be, Mom."

"If that's the truth, then I feel sorry for you," Kim joked. "Haven't you ever been to that swanky steakhouse owned by Evan Snow? Now, that's a place I'd rather be. Why don't you get yourself a date and go out?"

"Right. Like it's so easy to get a date," Jennifer quipped. She then eyed the clock on her phone and said, "She's two minutes late now."

"Jen..." Kim warned.

But there was no reason to stress. Just then, Kristine pulled Heather's car into the driveway, stopped the engine, and stepped out, jangling the keys as she went. As usual, she wore her fashionable, sleek-cut winter coat, which probably suited her just fine in New York City but clearly wasn't warm enough for Bar Harbor. She then skipped quickly up the driveway, up the porch steps, and prepared to knock on the door. Before she could, Jennifer opened the door.

"Oh! Hi!" Kristine smiled, embarrassed that both Kim and Jennifer looked at her from the foyer. "Am I late?"

"Not at all, honey," Kim said. "Jennifer was just leaving."

Jennifer eyed Kim sternly, then spoke to Kristine. "All of the doctors' numbers are on the fridge. You have mine, and of course, if you need anything else..."

"She knows to call 9-1-1," Kim quipped. "They teach you that in kindergarten." She then winked at Kristine, hoping the young woman wasn't too petrified of Kim's declining health.

"I think we'll be fine," Kristine tried to assure Jennifer, her voice wavering.

"We'll have fun," Kim added.

"That's what I'm afraid of," Jennifer said, rolling her eyes as she set out. "I love you, Mom. See you in about five hours?"

Kristine and Kim waited in the foyer to watch as Jennifer eased out of the driveway and drove down the road. There was a strange silence, proof that Kristine didn't feel very comfortable.

"Can I get you anything?" Kristine stuttered as her hands clasped together.

Kim waved her hand and turned her wheelchair back toward the living room. "I'm good! Really good."

"Something to eat? A snack?" Kristine followed Kim into the living room like a nervous dog.

"Jennifer just forced me to eat. At least, I think she did." Kim paused for a moment, thinking back over the previous few hours. Nearly every day, she found foggy parts of her mind, proof the medication the doctors had prescribed really did affect her short-term memory. "Anyway, I'm sure my body will tell me if I'm hungry again. We're well-stocked around here. Jennifer acts like a prepper on shopping trips, terrified we'll run out of things like pasta and cans of beans."

Kristine laughed appreciatively, her face open. She dropped onto the couch next to Kim and eyed the television, where a talk show host interviewed a mid-grade actress.

"Tell you the truth, I'm so bored of watching television," Kim said. "I don't understand how people sit around the house all day doing this on purpose."

"It's fun for a little while," Kristine said. "Like, when I feel particularly sad, sometimes it's good to binge-watch a TV show."

"Maybe the difference is you don't have to do that while I'm actually stuck here," Kim suggested.

Kristine's face was shadowed. "Yes. I'm sorry. Of course."

Kim felt guilty, as she hadn't wanted to make Kristine feel bad. "When was the last TV binge you had?"

Kristine winced. "After Patrick and I broke up, I spent a lot of time eating snacks and watching television. The world seemed to go on without me. I guess that's part of the reason why Bella dragged me here."

Suddenly, Kim grabbed the remote control, turned off the television, and wheeled her chair to the window. A beautiful orange sunlight shimmered across the rolling hills that were covered in snow, and she was overcome with the feeling that they needed to get out in it. She turned to catch Kristine's eye and tell her so, but Kristine was already slipping her arms into her coat sleeves.

"Oh, honey. That coat won't do," Kim insisted.

"What do you mean?"

"There has to be something thicker in the front closet. If you're going to live in Maine, you have to dress the part," Kim said.

Kristine laughed. "All right. I get the hint." She rushed to the front closet, where she drew out a very thick winter coat, one Kim had worn during her particularly frigid snowmobile outings. "What about this one?" She showed it off, putting it on and twisting her body this way and that.

"It's perfect. Better than haute couture," Kim joked.

The temperature was in the teens, but the sunlight across their cheeks was invigorating and kept them upbeat and alive. Kristine wheeled Kim along the small, paved road near Frenchman Bay, where they could take in the glow of the painfully chilly turquoise waters beneath a strange, if brief, blue-sky afternoon.

Although Kim loved her daughter and Heather to bits, she was grateful to be away from their prying eyes. Here, she could enjoy the pleasant and easy company of Kristine, who didn't pester her with questions about her short-term memory or how well she'd slept the previous night. Instead, Kristine seemed content to hear Kim's stories from the past, especially those about the men in her life. As Kim's short-term memory was currently blotchy, she had nothing but memories right now, and she poured them out easily, overwhelmed with the details she could share.

"You've really lived such a life," Kristine said, her voice dreamy.

"You're well on your way," Kim told her. "For all my exciting stories, I have double the number of stories where things didn't go quite my way." She gestured toward the wheelchair and added, "Take this situation, for example."

About a mile from the house, Kristine stopped the chair to grab the water bottles she'd stocked beneath the wheelchair. Kim drank greedily, watching Kristine's expression as she studied the sky above. Truthfully, in the previous ten or so minutes, their blue sky had been defeated, and thick, bulbous gray and black clouds had emerged, pressing down upon them.

Kristine leafed through the pockets of her big winter coat and removed her phone. A second later, she showed Kim the screen, which advertised a **WINTER SNOW WARNING** for the area of Bar Harbor and the Acadia Mountains.

"Huh!" Kim laughed, her eyes toward the clouds. "I never would have expected that a half-hour ago."

Kristine was clearly nervous. She stepped around to the back of Kim's wheelchair and said, "We'd better get back." Meanwhile, Kim scanned the weather report and said, "Looks like we'll get anywhere between six inches to a foot."

"You're kidding!" Kristine was shocked.

"You've been out of Maine too long, my girl," Kim said. "This is the weather I live for."

Kristine tried to laugh, but she was clearly nervous, wanting to get Kim back to safety before the snow began to flutter down. About ten minutes before the front porch, the first of the snowflakes flattened across Kim's nose, and Kim laughed, feeling euphoric.

"Isn't it funny we're so panicked about a little snow?" Kim said, her palms outstretched so that the snow melted across them. "Come on, Kristine. Look at it! It's gorgeous."

Kristine continued to push Kim's wheelchair along Frenchman Bay and then rightward up the road that led to her driveway. When they approached the little house, Kim's heart leaped into her throat. There, parked in the snow in her front yard, was a very familiar snowmobile. She hadn't seen it in what seemed like years.

"Who's here?" Kristine asked under her breath, clearly exhausted from racing the snow.

"Robbie?" Kim scanned the front yard before finding him on the front porch, all bundled up in his winter garb with a big plastic Tupperware container in his hands. He waved a sturdy hand and smiled through his thick New England beard, which he'd had since Kim had met him thirty-five years ago.

"Robbie?" Kristine muttered curiously as she wheeled Kim the rest of the way to the front porch, where Jennifer had installed a ramp for the chair.

A mix of pleasure and embarrassment warmed Kim's cheeks. Overwhelmed, she raised both arms and gripped one of Robbie's hands with both of hers. Just as ever, he was handsome, shy, and eager, with his eyes just as bright as they were in her memories.

"I just heard what happened," Robbie stuttered.

"That's right. You spent a few months out of town, didn't you?" Kim asked.

"With my daughter in Florida," Robbie replied. His eyes narrowed with concern. "Wow, Kim. What happened out on that road?"

Kim tried to laugh, although it didn't sound happy. "Your guess is as good as mine."

"You were always the best rider I knew," Robbie offered, referring to their long-ago trips— back when Robbie had been married, and so had Kim. They'd traveled in groups of eight, racing through the trails and stopping in small villages for hearty meals that cut out the chill.

"Kristine, this is Robbie," Kim introduced, suddenly remembering Kristine was still behind her. "He's an old friend and lives just about a half-mile away."

"The closest thing you have to a neighbor over here," Robbie reminded her, shaking Kristine's hand.

"Kristine is my niece's daughter," Kim explained. "I think I mentioned I have a long-lost niece through my estranged sister?"

Robbie nodded in recognition. "That has got to be one of the crazier stories I've ever heard." He then dropped Kristine's handshake and lifted the Tupperware, in which he'd placed several helpings of homemade Shepherd's Pie.

"Oh! I always adored Shepherd's Pie!" Kim was momentarily overwhelmed with happiness.

"I remember," he said, his smile widening.

For a moment, Kim wasn't sure what to do. On the one hand, she felt totally foolish, there in her wheelchair as this handsome man towered over her. On the other hand, he looked at her with those beautiful, knowing eyes, as though she was the only woman in the world.

"Why don't you come inside?" Kristine interjected, coming in to save the day. "We can heat up the Shepherd's Pie and watch the snow."

"Oh, I don't want to intrude." Robbie took a step back.

"Nonsense," Kim said. "We'd love the company." Her smile was so huge it made her face ache.

Chapter Twelve

Kim's kitchen window displayed a gorgeous view of the snowfall. Each snowflake seemed bigger than the next, coming down quickly to pile a thick layer over the window edges and the porch steps. Kristine set Kim up at the kitchen table with a mug of hot tea and offered Robbie a domestic beer, which he accepted gladly. As Kristine buzzed around, tending to the tea and the Shepherd's Pie, she was aware of how little Robbie and Kim acknowledged Kristine at all. They seemed enthralled with one another, their eyes locked as they traded stories from the previous few months. For brief moments, Kim seemed so youthful and vibrant that Kristine nearly forgot that she'd been in a coma at all.

"My daughter is bent on moving me down to Florida," Robbie explained, sipping his beer.

"Oh, of course, she is. That Nina. She was always such a diva!" Kim laughed gently. "Every time I saw her back in the old days, she had another scheme in mind. One minute, she wanted to be an actress. The next, a horse trainer."

"I remember." Robbie's eyes glinted. "It was a miracle I

convinced her to go to college here in Maine. I got four more good years out of her being close by. Of course, that was around the time her mother passed." He dropped his gaze for a moment. "For once in her life, she wanted to stay close to home."

Kristine turned and gently scooped Shepherd's Pie from the Tupperware and onto a baking sheet. With the oven preheated, she slipped the baking sheet onto the iron rack. The air in the kitchen was heavy with the memory of Robbie's clear loss— a wife he'd loved, who'd died too young.

"It was a terrible time," Kim breathed. "I can't imagine it's been easy for you over the years."

Robbie lifted his beer. "You understand loss just as well as I do."

"It's a symptom of being alive this long," Kim said. "Loss is just a part of life. I'm grateful to have made it as long as I have, but goodness, I still miss the ones I've lost."

Kristine's heart dropped in her chest. It was strange to listen to these stories, to know that no matter how much loss she'd already experienced, there was still more where that came from. *How did anyone pick themselves up and go on?*

"Have you given any thought to moving to Florida, then?" Kim asked, helping them from the silence.

"I've considered it. I even have a pro and con list written out." Robbie chuckled. "But the thing is, I'm a man from Maine. I don't know if I know how to be anything else. Besides, Florida people are nice and all, but sometimes I think they're too nice. Is it fake?"

Kim laughed. "People from the south are a different breed, that's for sure. Oh, but they'd take you into their communities easily. You're just about the most likable guy around Bar Harbor."

Kristine eyed Kim, surprised at how openly flirtatious she was. Robbie blushed and tried to stutter his way into another topic of conversation. With the snow piling down outside, Kristine half-expected Robbie to say he had to go on home. Still, he remained at the table, unwilling to leave Kim after so long apart.

Shortly after, Kristine served the steaming Shepherd's Pie on beautifully painted china and poured Kim a glass of non-alcoholic wine, herself a glass of real wine, and grabbed another beer for Robbie. Together, they sat at the kitchen table and gazed at the winter wonderland outside the window, their plates heavy with Shepherd's Pie.

"It's like we're in a snow globe." Kristine spoke for the first time in over forty minutes, as she'd been too preoccupied with listening to Robbie and Kim.

"That car of yours is heavy with snow already," Kim warned.

Robbie slid his knife and fork through the Shepherd's Pie, his brow furrowed. "I think it's best you stay the night here until they clear the roads in the morning. According to the forecast, the snow should quit around one or so. And you know how people in Maine are about cleaning the roads."

"They're quick," Kim chimed in, smiling her beautiful smile at first Robbie, then Kristine. She was clearly pleased that Robbie cared so much about Kristine's safety. "Of course, Kristine knows all about quick snow clean-ups. Kristine grew up in Maine. But we've lost her to the big city."

Robbie tilted his head, interested. "Which big city is that?"

"The biggest," Kim spoke for Kristine. "The Big Apple! Goodness, when I lived there, that city nearly ate me alive."

"I almost forgot about that time of your life," Robbie said, puffing his chest out. He was clearly impressed. "You were always more adventurous than anyone else I knew." He turned to lock eyes with Kristine as he added, "Kim was always pressing our snowmobile party to go faster, further. The others would say, 'No, please! Kim! We need to rest! It's too cold!' But

Kim always called them sissies, zipped up her snowmobile suit, and stomped out into the snow." His smile was enormous, showing teeth that he'd taken care of well over the years. "Your husband was never sure what to do with you, Kimmy."

Kristine's eyes widened. *Had Robbie really just said that?* Her eyes danced from Kim to Robbie and back again, mesmerized. She felt like she was on a dating show for people over seventy.

"Well. Eventually, I figured out what to do with him," Kim joked, pointing her thumb toward the door.

Robbie winced, but Kim waved it off. "The divorce wasn't such a big deal. The hardest part of it was getting him to pick up the last of his stuff. I had a metric ton of hunting equipment in the garage for a good five years before he finally remembered to come get it."

Robbie laughed, clearly pleased. "Do you hear from him often?"

Kim shrugged. "Here and there. We share children, grand-children, and now, a great-grandchild, so we have plenty to talk about that has nothing to do with our failed relationship."

"That's a rare thing. So many of my divorced friends want nothing to do with their ex-spouses," Robbie said with his fork lifted.

Kim took a sip of her non-alcoholic wine and studied him. Kristine leaned forward, anticipating another juicy moment of flirtation.

"That makes me sad," Kim began. "How many decades of my life did I spend with him? How many beautiful moments did we share? Countless. Just because we fell out of love doesn't mean that I will ever hate him. I still treasure every-thing that happened. I still treasure the fact that he exists."

Robbie raised his glass of wine, his eyes shining. "I've never heard a more beautiful sentiment."

Kim laughed, trying to clear the air of how serious she'd

made it. "I'm getting soft in my old age, I suppose. That, and I spent an entire month in a coma. Or so they tell me."

Robbie's face was grave. "Did it feel like you were gone a long time?"

Kim considered this. "It's funny. I wish I could compare it to another experience. Like, when you sleep for ten hours, you know that your consciousness went somewhere else. Right?"

Robbie and Kristine both nodded, captivated by this woman who'd spent so much time "somewhere else."

"I suppose it's sort of like that. Except when I woke up, I couldn't speak. I couldn't use my muscles. Even my brain is a bit foggy from the medicine." Kim's face was shadowed with sorrow. "I know it'll pass. Everything always does. But it's been a consistent struggle, one I don't want to talk about often, as I know it makes my daughter very sad."

Robbie reached across the table and draped his hand over Kim's. Kristine averted her gaze and sipped her wine, feeling like a third wheel. Somehow, she sensed this comfort was exactly the kind Kim had needed all along.

After the Shepherd's Pie, Kim took another round of medicine and admitted she needed a nap. She sounded sheepish when she said it, as though she didn't want to show any weakness.

"Kim, you need your rest!" Robbie insisted, jumping up from the table to clear the plates. "Don't let me keep you from your bed. We need you to heal up quickly so you can get back to your wild and carefree life."

Kim blushed, then yawned, already wheeling herself away from the table. Robbie followed after her, eager to help her with whatever she needed. Kristine was pleased as she watched the two. The thought of helping Kim into her bed from the wheelchair had frightened her for hours. Robbie was a welcome relief for both of them.

A few minutes later, Robbie stepped out of Kim's bedroom, closed the door behind him, and headed for the door.

"Robbie! Wait a second. Would you like me to wash your Tupperware? You could take it home tonight." Kristine palmed her neck, feeling anxious. It was strange to be "in charge" in a house she wasn't familiar with.

"Oh, don't worry about that. I have mountains of Tupperware." Robbie smiled again, adjusting his winter coat over his shoulder. He then opened the front door and peered through the swirling snow at his snowmobile. "You promise me you won't try to drive home tonight?"

"I don't think I'd make it out of the driveway," Kristine said.

"Kim has my number if you need anything at all. I'm just a five-minute drive away," Robbie explained. "Food. Wine. Anything at all. I hate that I didn't hear about Kim's accident until this week. Somebody should have told me. Kim, at least, should have texted about it!"

"She's had a lot on her mind. I'm sure she didn't want to worry you," Kristine said softly.

Robbie's face twisted with a mix of emotions. He then locked eyes with Kristine and said, "Just let her know that I'm here. No matter what she needs."

With the door closed tightly against the frigid evening, Kristine sat wrapped in a blanket on the couch and flicked through the television. The weather channel showed the snow front, which was still very dense over Bar Harbor over the next two to three hours.

Stewing in loneliness, Kristine dialed her mother's number.

"Hi, honey! Quite a storm out there. How are you holding up?" Heather sounded chipper. Kristine could practically see her at the Keating House kitchen counter, a glass of wine lifted as onions caramelized in the skillet.

Kristine's heart lifted at the sound of her mother's voice. "Needless to say, I don't think I'll make it back tonight."

"I didn't think so. Is everything okay over there? Are you handling Kim all right?"

"She's fine. A neighbor friend of hers came by with a Tupperware of Shepherd's Pie. We all sat together and ate."

"Yum! I love Shepherd's Pie. Who was she?"

"A he, actually. His name is Robbie, and he seems to have a real big crush on Aunt Kim."

Heather gasped with excitement. "Thank goodness you're in Bar Harbor. I needed this kind of gossip to get me through the cold winter."

Kristine laughed and went on to explain, "They both knew each other's exes. His died several years ago, which is quite sad. But Kim was quick to tell him what a wonderful woman she was."

"Oh. That's sad." Heather's voice softened. Probably, she thought of her own loss, Kristine's father.

"But seriously, Mom," Kristine tried to lift the mood. "You should have seen the way these two looked at each other. It was steamy."

Heather giggled, then paused for a moment. "Oh, your sister just walked in. She's got paint all over her face. You want to say hello?"

Kristine laughed and agreed, grateful to hear her twin's voice. Over the next several minutes, Bella blabbered about all things painting, Florian, and her upcoming gallery show in the city. "I swear, if Florian saw how crazy I look right now, he'd break up with me on the spot."

"Don't be silly. It's all a part of your artist charm," Kristine teased.

When Kristine got off the phone, she poured herself another glass of wine and again cuddled up on the couch, watching as the white snow flattened against the living room windows. She felt cocooned by frigid weather, by thickening snow.

Habit led her to open her social media. It was something she did all the time, a way to pass the time. Her thumb flicked through photographs of her friends in the city, sipping expensive cocktails and bragging about their jobs on Wall Street or in internet companies. In the photos, her friends looked beautiful and carefree, without any of the baggage Kristine knew they had. So far away from them, it was easy for Kristine to pretend that they didn't have that baggage at all.

After about ten minutes, Kristine stumbled upon an article from *The Wall Street Journal*, one that shocked her to her core.

CEO Richard Coswald Sued for Sexual Harassment

Kristine shot straight up from the couch, no longer cozy. She clicked on the article and read, feeling angrier than she'd been in her life.

The article read:

CEO Richard Coswald is widely regarded as one of the most cutthroat businessmen in the industry. Recently, an employee at his company, The Coswald Group, stepped forward to accuse both Coswald and his personal assistant, Patrick Lockhard, of sexual harassment and inappropriate commentary in the workplace.

Kristine's jaw dropped. She reread the paragraph, feeling her heartbeat pick up. She then texted a friend, Veronica, who she'd gone to business school with and who understood the ins and outs of the business world.

KRISTINE: Hey! I just read this article in the Journal. Do you know what happened?

VERONICA: Omg. Everyone is talking about it. Apparently, Coswald wanted to sleep with a young woman at the office— but Patrick got to her first. Richard was angry about this and began to berate

Patrick about it during an all-male staff meeting. Some of the staff members leaked this information to the young woman, and she promptly pressed charges.

VERONICA: Apparently, Richard was very creepy with her otherwise. Grabbing her and demanding that she stay longer after-hours.

VERONICA: Anyway, I'm so glad you're out of there! Both of those guys are creeps!

VERONICA: No doubt that there will be a settlement, and both Patrick and Richard will get away with it, though.

VERONICA: Anyway, are you back in the city? We should get drinks! I'd love to hear what you're doing now.

Kristine's mouth was terribly dry. Unaware of her body, she threw her phone across the couch, burrowed her face in her hands, and began to weep.

This was the job and boss she'd given her life to.

This was the relationship she'd thought would be hers forever.

What had she been thinking? Could she ever trust her opinion of people again? Could she ever fall in love again, since she knew this feeling of shame lurked on the other side?

How could she have been so stupid?

Chapter Thirteen

Fat dollops of snow melted gently on the windows of Kim's bedroom. Outside, the last of the evening light had dimmed to darkness, and with it, another day was through. Kim assessed her legs, her abdomen, and the weight of her arms and found that her body felt lighter and freer than it had since the accident. It was as though the heat from the Shepherd's Pie, the laughter from her conversation with Robbie, and the sharp chill of the fresh air had combined to form the perfect medicine.

Jennifer had placed a very small Christmas bell on the side table of Kim's room, which Kim now lifted to jangle. She hated doing this, as she felt annoying, but it was more practical than yelling, she supposed. Kristine appeared in the doorway a few seconds later, her eyes lined pink. She'd been crying, that was clear, but Kim wasn't sure if Kristine felt up to talking about it. The poor girl had been through a lot.

"How was your nap?" Kristine asked, stepping up to adjust Kim's wheelchair next to her bed.

"I was out like a light," Kim said, lifting herself up on her elbows. This was something she hadn't been able to do even a few days ago, and she relished it. "I take it Robbie's long gone?"

"I couldn't keep him company, I'm afraid. He only wanted you." Kristine's eyes, though still sad, twinkled with goodwill.

Heat rushed up Kim's chest and neck. "Oh, no. That's just Robbie. He flirts with everyone."

"I have a feeling that's not true," Kristine insisted. "He looked at you like you were the sun, the moon, and the stars put together."

Gently, Kristine helped Kim roll herself onto the wheelchair, where Kim positioned her feet on the footrests and laced her fingers through her messy curls. "I'm sorry you have to see this. A little old lady, fresh out of bed."

"Don't be silly," Kristine said. "You should see how I look when I get up in the morning. It's not pretty."

In the living room, Kristine set Kim up at a little table with a glass of non-alcoholic wine, a chocolate chip cookie, and a glass of water. Kristine poured herself a glass of real wine and curled up on the couch directly next to Kim, urging her to flick through the television channels.

The coziness of being tucked away in the warmth of your house with a good movie on and the snow swirling outside was unparalleled. Although Kim hated her wheelchair and hated her foggy, medicine-laced mind, she wasn't too messed up to appreciate this. She eyed Kristine with a soft smile and said, "I hope you're up for some romantic comedies."

Kristine's very sad eyes opened wider. "It's exactly what I need right now."

Kim hunted through the film and TV show apps that Jennifer had set up on her television before she finally discovered a classic— When Harry Met Sally. Kristine admitted she adored the film, saying, "It takes place in the eighties or something? But I swear relationships between men and women are no different now than back then."

Kim laughed. "I don't think relationships between men and women will ever change. Women don't really understand men, and men don't really understand women. Unfortunately, for most of us, we're stuck with each other."

Kristine wrinkled her nose and sipped her wine, captivated by the opening sequence of the film. After a few minutes, as a beautiful and young Meg Ryan leaped into a junky car with Billy Crystal to begin the rest of her life, Kristine suddenly said, "My ex-boyfriend is being charged with sexual harassment in the workplace."

Kim's lips parted with surprise. She paused the film and turned to watch Kristine, whose face crumpled as her tears fell unhindered. All Kim wanted in the world was to jump up from her wheelchair and go hug the poor girl.

"My gosh. I'm assuming you're talking about Patrick?" Kim whispered, remembering the terrible boy from New Year's Eve.

Kristine nodded, hiccupping with sadness. "Apparently, he and my ex-boss were really cruel to this young woman at my old workplace. I can't even begin to fathom that. Yes, my ex-boss was terrible. But Patrick? I considered marrying Patrick! I brought him home for crying out loud!" She sputtered.

Kim felt helpless, watching her great-niece fall apart. Never in Kim's life had she felt as betrayed as Kristine felt now.

"Kristine? Listen to me." Kim spoke with finality.

Kristine sniffed and opened her eyes, surprised.

"You are and have always been better than that boy," Kim said firmly. "I know you loved him. But you're not the first beautiful and talented woman in the world who has fallen for a terrible guy. It's happened to so many of us. What matters most is you got out of there. What matters most is he showed you who he really was, and you ran."

Kristine's lower lip bounced. "All I wanted to do was love

him. All I wanted to do was build our careers and our lives side-by-side."

Kim set her jaw. "I know that, honey. But this man wasn't the one. Not for you, and not for any other woman, not until he gets his head on straight."

Kristine lifted her eyes to the television screen, where Billy Crystal was frozen, wearing one of his classic eighties' sweaters.

"A friend texted to say Patrick and my ex-boss would probably get away with it," Kristine whispered. "I hate that she's right. All they have to do is throw money at the situation, and it goes away."

"That's heinous," Kim muttered. "But I suppose it's the way the city works."

"It made me second-guess my career choice," Kristine said. "Why would I want to throw myself back in the lion's den? Why would I want to climb up a corporate ladder, knowing that men like that lurk in every corner? Maybe I'm too idealistic. Maybe I belong in a silly romantic comedy with Meg Ryan and Billy Crystal."

Kim lifted her finger. "First of all, *When Harry Met Sally* is not silly. It's an honest portrait of friendship, romance, and the confusion of being alive."

Kristine laughed gently, color returning to her cheeks.

"Second of all, being too idealistic isn't a bad thing. It just means you have a dream for a better world. Why not work for whatever that is?" Kim asked.

The film continued as the snow continued to billow outside. Kim sipped her non-alcoholic wine, feeling so content with Kristine there— a woman who reminded her of herself and the aimlessness of being twenty-three.

After the first time-jump in the film, Kristine turned her head to regard Kim and asked, "So, have you and Robbie dated before?"

Kim laughed with surprise. She paused the film again, sensing it was her time for honesty. "Robbie was married for decades. We were just casual friends, nothing more. My husband used to drink beer at his. They went fishing and hunting, the sorts of things men do together. I don't think they were ever very close. They certainly didn't have heart-to-hearts like us."

Kristine smiled.

"After my divorce and Robbie's wife's death, the dynamic between us changed slightly. I noticed he hung around a little longer than I expected and that he touched my shoulder as we spoke. We've both been out of the dating game for ages— I don't think either of us would know how to begin if we tried."

Kim eyed her legs in the wheelchair, remembering the months of physical therapy in her future.

"He doesn't care about that," Kristine interjected, as though she'd read Kim's mind. "He's so glad you're okay."

Kim shrugged gently. "Losing his wife nearly destroyed him. Recently, I almost passed away, too. I don't want to bring that man any more pain. He's had enough."

Kristine's smile softened. "But Kim. You said it yourself, didn't you? That it's a blessing to live this long, even though your life is lined with loss? Don't you think Robbie is open to something new? And don't you think you owe it to yourself to try?"

Chapter Fourteen

Kristine slept like a log in the guest room. Thick, hand-knitted blankets wrapped around her, and fluffy pillows cradled her tired head. At various times through the night, she woke up to the memory of Patrick's sexual harassment lawsuit— and she clutched the blankets, weeping until exhaustion took over and allowed her to sleep. New York City was graciously miles and miles away. It was like a monster she'd left behind.

The next morning, an eggshell blue sky stretched for miles and miles above the glittering snow. Kristine and Kim sat in the kitchen and gazed out at it, mesmerized at the stillness of the land and the glorious sky. It was true that in the city, Kristine so often missed the bigness of the sky, as it was normally punctuated with skyscrapers. Once upon a time, she'd thought skyscrapers were beautiful. What had she been thinking?

Kristine made coffee and cinnamon rolls, and together, Kim and Kristine feasted, warming their insides as the radio played Shania Twain, Alanis Morrissette, and Ace of Base. Kristine checked online to see that the roads had been cleared in downtown Bar Harbor, but that the crew hadn't made it quite this far out yet. They would soon, probably by late afternoon.

"Jennifer's texting me every three minutes," Kim complained with a laugh. "She thinks I'm probably dead by now."

"She doesn't trust me, I take it?" Kristine asked, taking their plates to the dishwasher.

"She doesn't trust anyone," Kim affirmed. "But she needed time off from me. I love her to pieces, but she can be over-bearing— and I don't take kindly to that. I might have snapped at her a few times."

"You've been through a lot. You're allowed to be in a bad mood here and there."

A knock came from the front door. Kristine snapped the dishwasher closed and hustled to answer it, knowing it could only be one person. Sure enough, when she opened it, Robbie stood, broad and firm and all bundled up in the doorway. In his hands, he held another Tupperware, this time filled with brownies and blondies. His smile was welcoming and warm.

"Good morning! Quite a storm last night!" His voice echoed through the house.

"Uh oh. He brought more food, Kim!" Kristine took the Tupperware and opened the door wider so he could enter.

He kicked off his boots and removed his coat, which he hung up to dry. "The snow is beautiful out there. The drive from my place was a dream."

"I can only imagine!" Kim called from the kitchen. "Now, · get in here, so I don't have to yell across the house."

Robbie cackled and practically skipped into the kitchen. Kristine had never seen a grown man skip like that before. She followed after him, watching as he dipped down to hug Kim hello.

"Pour yourself a mug of coffee and sit down," Kim ordered.

"Aye, aye, captain." Robbie reached for a mug in the cabinet and joined Kim at the table. His smile waned slightly as he said, "I'm afraid I have some bad news."

Kim arched her brow. "Uh oh. I don't like the sound of that."

"It's nothing serious," he explained. "But the oak next to your house on the south side lost a limb in the snowstorm. It's on your roof, threatening to smash into the bay window on the other side if we don't take immediate action."

Kim nodded. "I can call a tree guy tomorrow, I suppose."

"Don't worry yourself. I already have my guy on his way," Robbie explained.

"Your guy! You have a tree guy?" Kim sipped her coffee, pleased.

"I have a guy for everything," Robbie said. "He's got great equipment, a snowmobile, and not much else to do today. I told him I would pay him a bit extra if he could get the job done by the afternoon."

"Oh, Robbie. You don't have to do this," Kim insisted.

"I'm just being neighborly. Trying to make up for lost time after missing your accident." Robbie furrowed his brow. "I should have been here to help out."

Kim shook her head, at a loss for words. Finally, she managed, "What's this I hear about more food?"

Robbie's smile widened. He reached for the Tupperware, which Kristine still had in her hands, and showed off the selection of brownies and blondies, which he'd baked up the previous evening when he'd been "bored."

"I hope you're bored all winter long, Robbie," Kim said. She selected a blondie and broke it apart in the center. It was thick, almost fudge-like in texture. After she took a small bite, she moaned and said, "You're very talented. You'd sweep the awards on those baking TV shows."

Robbie laughed and took a brownie before glancing back toward Kristine. "Eat up, Kristine."

"We just ate cinnamon rolls," Kristine protested, her hand across her stomach. "I don't know if I have any room."

"Don't be silly," Kim insisted. "If there's ever a time to over-indulge in sweets, it's today."

As Kim and Robbie began to discuss people and things Kristine didn't know anything about, Kristine sat at the kitchen table and took a blondie from the container. She remembered several weeks ago when Patrick had begun yet another low-carb diet, his sights set on a swimsuit season that was still five months away. "I can't believe some people's eating habits. I mean, don't they know how bad sugar is?" he'd said, stabbing his fork through a kale salad.

"Honey," Kim interrupted Robbie, her eyes narrowed. "You're supposed to eat the blondie. Not stare at it."

Kristine tried to laugh, her heart thundering. With both Robbie and Kim's eyes upon her, she couldn't do anything but lift the blondie, close her eyes, and take a bite. The fudge-y texture and warm, buttery taste was overwhelming. She clapped her hand over her mouth, her eyes wide open.

"Uh oh. You destroyed her," Kim said with a laugh.

Kristine shook her head, both embarrassed and pleased. "People would pay six bucks each for a blondie like this in New York City."

Robbie shook his head. "Charging money would take all the fun out of it for me."

Kristine cocked her head, surprised at this answer. In her city life, people did anything for a quick buck. Before she could think of something else to say, a knock at the door saved her. She popped up to answer it, followed quickly by Robbie.

"I think it's my tree guy," he explained.

Kristine got to the door first and opened it, feeling a sense of responsibility for Kim's house. To her surprise, the man at the door was familiar to her— all bundled up, his handsome face wrapped in wild curls and his blue eyes shining.

"Carter?" Kristine's voice was high-pitched and girlish.

Carter kicked his head back, startled. "Kristine? What are you doing here?"

He was just as handsome as he'd been the other day. After the chilly snowmobile ride, his cheeks and nose were cherry red, which added a hint of adorableness to his attractiveness. Kristine's knees wobbled. Behind her, Robbie laughed good-naturedly, noticing the bizarre air between them.

"I take it you two know each other?"

Kristine stepped back, putting two and two together. "Bare-ly," she explained. She then eyed Carter to add, "You're the tree guy?"

"My friends call me 'The Tree Guy,'" Carter joked. "But you can call me Carter if you want."

"Naw. I'd love to call you 'Tree Guy.'" Kristine couldn't stop smiling. Was she flirting? "You want to come in for a cup of coffee? We have plenty of blondies and brownies to go around."

Carter eyed Robbie. He looked vibrant, as though he'd just received very good news. "I think I'll get started on removing that limb first. Best to get the work done first and celebrate with sweets later."

"A wise man," Robbie affirmed, grabbing his coat. "I'll help however I can."

When Kristine breezed back into the kitchen, she found Kim wearing a funny smile.

"What?" Kristine demanded with her hands on her hips.

Kim clucked her tongue. It was obvious she'd heard every-thing. "Oh. Nothing."

"Kim..." Kristine warned.

Kim lifted her hands. "It seems to me I'm not the only one with a flirtation. That's all."

Kristine rolled her eyes and plopped back down in the kitchen chair. Attraction to Carter and adrenaline from the snowstorm made her especially loose-lipped. "He came by the house the other day to tell me his younger brother stole from the candy shop. He handed over bags and bags of cookies and candy, which my family has had very little trouble getting through." Kristine giggled, then added, her voice more serious, "His brother gets in a lot of trouble. It sounds like Carter is the only one who cares if TJ graduates from high school or stays out of prison at all."

"Ah. The Bilson boys?" Kim nodded as her eyes filled with sorrow.

"You know them?"

"There are people in this community who were given the short end of the stick," Kim breathed. "But the older Bilson boy, your Carter, is a proud one. He won't accept help from anyone."

Kristine's heart filled with pride, although she wasn't sure why. There was something about a man who wanted to do everything himself. It was such a contrast to Patrick, who'd been given everything as a child.

"If there's something between you and Carter, you could do a whole lot worse," Kim added knowingly. "Why not have a little fun this winter? You deserve it."

After the tree limb was cleared, Robbie and Carter stomped off their boots, hung their coats to dry, and sat in the kitchen in their socks to enjoy hot coffee and brownies. Carter announced that the roads were nearly cleared, which meant that Kristine would probably be able to head home soon. On cue, Jennifer called Kim to say that she was about to brave the roads to come back to her.

"My doting daughter is on her way," Kim announced with a laugh. "She doesn't know how to leave me alone for more than a day. Bless her."

"I suppose that's what love is," Robbie kidded.

For a strange moment, Carter and Kristine locked eyes over

the table. Carter had a piece of brownie lifted in his very large and capable hand. He looked like he wanted to say something, something that mattered. But instead, he dropped his gaze and left Kristine wanting more.

"I haven't seen your daughter in ages," Robbie said. "Mind if I stick around and say hello?"

Kim's cheeks glowed with surprise. "You'd be doing me a favor, getting between me and the line of fire. All these questions! Did I take my medication? Did I get enough rest? Am I drinking enough fluids? Good grief! I've kept myself alive this long, haven't I?"

Everyone at the table laughed.

"She sounds like me with my little brother," Carter explained. "I hear myself nagging him all the time, and I think, 'Is that really me?' I used to be cool! I used to be fun! Now, I'm just boring and responsible."

"Welcome to adulthood," Robbie said, lifting his mug of coffee.

"I don't subscribe to the theory that adulthood is boring," Kim corrected. "With that said, I always drink enough water. It keeps me youthful." She winked.

After Jennifer arrived, she bustled around the house, tending to messes that didn't exist. Kristine gathered her things, hugged Kim goodbye, and headed for the front door, where Carter remained, waiting for her. He blushed like a teenager waiting for a girl at her locker.

Kristine bundled up in the coat Kim had lent her and packed her city one in her backpack. Carter pressed open the door to hold it open for her, and she passed through, thanking him. Outside, the blue sky had darkened to a soft gray.

"You headed home?" she asked him as they walked toward her mother's car. She jangled her keys in her pocket.

"Guess so." Carter smiled at her. *Was he nervous?* "I hope

TJ hasn't gotten himself into any trouble today. Then again, most places downtown were closed. Not much to rob from."

Kristine wrinkled her nose. "It sounds exhausting."

"It is." Carter palmed the back of his neck, watching as Kristine slung her backpack into the back seat and opened the front door. "Listen. Um."

Kristine turned, so that her nose was only a few inches from his. Her heart beat quickly, like a rabbit's. "What's up?"

Carter laughed, embarrassed. "This is going to sound crazy."

"I'm sure it won't." The other things Kristine had learned over the previous twenty-four hours were probably a lot crazier.

"Well. Would you maybe like to grab dinner with me sometime?" Carter stuttered. "Like, on a date? In case it isn't obvious that I'm asking you out." He smiled that handsome smile and his dimple went deeper than ever before.

Kristine's lips parted with surprise. Back when Patrick had first asked her out, she'd wanted to do backflips around her and Bella's living room. This felt different, softer.

"Oh. That sounds nice." Kristine smiled, unsure of how she really felt.

Carter's smile widened. "Great. Really great." He nodded a little too quickly, then produced his phone to collect her phone number. She entered it in as chilly New England winds whizzed past her ears. "I'll text you tonight."

When Carter sat on his snowmobile, he lifted his sturdy hand in the air and started the engine. Kristine remained in the front seat of her mother's car with her heart in her throat. Her stomach stirred with a mix of gladness and dread. What on earth was she doing? *And was it really the way to a happy ending?*

Chapter Fifteen

Several nights later, Kristine zipped herself into a tight-fitting black dress and shimmied in the mirror, analyzing every angle. Behind her, Bella was strewn across Kristine's bed at the Keating House with paint in her hair and fuzzy socks on her feet. Despite her scumminess, she had the audacity to say, "That's not the look for tonight, Kris."

Kristine puffed out her cheeks, turned, and demanded, "What's wrong with it?"

Bella raised one shoulder. "He's taking you for burgers and beers. You're dressed for a night out in SoHo."

Kristine knew Bella was right. She was accustomed to date night with Patrick, when she was expected to look the part of a beautiful and successful counterpart to Patrick's brilliance. Tonight, she was going out on a date with Carter, The Tree Guy from Bar Harbor, who probably owned two button-down shirts and a suit for weddings. She couldn't wear couture, even if she had gotten it second-hand.

Bella jumped from the bed and walked to Kristine's closet,

where she shifted through jackets, skirts, sweaters, and blouses. "You have so much business wear," she teased.

"Yeah? Well, the first rule in the business world is you have to dress the part."

"You're not in the business world, baby. You're in Bar Harbor." Bella winked as she lifted a light pink cardigan from its hanger. "What about this with a jean skirt and a pair of high boots? It's flirty and fabulous with a bit of an, 'Oh, I just threw this on' vibe."

Kristine hadn't worn something so simple and easy for a night out since high school, maybe. Slowly, she buttoned the cardigan and the skirt and zipped the boots up her calves, feeling as though she'd donned a costume.

"Oh, it's perfect!" Bella cooed. "Mom! Come see Kristine!"

Heather and Nicole rushed into the bedroom, both effervescent about Kristine's upcoming date with a local.

"You're adorable," Nicole affirmed.

Heather tilted her head, understanding that this look was very different for Kristine. She wrapped a dark strand of hair around Kristine's ear and said, "The only question is this. Do you feel good in these clothes?"

Kristine thought about this for a moment, glancing at herself in the mirror. "They're more comfortable than anything I would have picked for myself."

Bella beamed. "You have to feel comfortable to let someone get to know you, Kris. I think it's the number one rule."

Kristine's heart felt bruised. Bella seemed to suggest that Kristine had never allowed Patrick to know her, not in a real sense. Did this make Kristine bad at dating and love?

Before she could question it, the downstairs doorbell rang.

"He's here!" Nicole sang.

"Oh gosh. I can't believe how nervous I am." Kristine wrinkled her nose and reached for her coat, the fancy one she normally wore.

"Good luck, honey. Just be yourself," Heather reminded her.

Kristine shot her mother a dark look. "That's exactly what I shouldn't be."

Bella, Nicole, and Heather hissed at once. "What are you talking about?"

"Don't take that attitude with you," Bella warned.

Kristine breathed deeply. "I'm sorry. As I said. I'm nervous." She paused for a moment, listening downstairs as Aunt Casey greeted Carter warmly and said Kristine would be down soon. "I love you all. Thank you for the support."

"We love you, too! Remember, we'll be here when you get home. We can pour wine and talk about everything," Bella affirmed, chasing Kristine down the hallway. "All the bad points and all the good."

* * *

Carter had driven his snowmobile to pick Kristine up. Kristine laughed as he positioned a snowmobile helmet on the crown of her head, grinning sheepishly. This was what it meant to date Bar Harbor boys, she supposed. She helped him shove the helmet the rest of the way down, surprised at how pleased she was as he buckled it under her chin. He really was charming, caring, and very handsome. And it was true what Aunt Kim had said. It was time for her to have a little fun.

Kristine wrapped her arms around Carter's waist, gripping a little harder than she'd meant to.

"Are you scared?" Carter teased.

Kristine's voice was high-pitched. "No! Never," she lied, loosening her grip.

"Don't worry. I'm no daredevil. I'll take it nice and slow."

The wind was sharp and jagged across Kristine's cheeks and forehead. They whipped downtown easily, where Carter parked the snowmobile alongside a string of other snowmobiles. This was the way Bar Harbor residents got around best. If Kristine planned to stick around, she'd had better get used to it.

The burger place Carter had picked was a quaint place with graffiti on the walls, televisions in the corners, and a twelve-tap of craft beers. The waiters and waitresses were around their age, with intricate tattoos and an easy air to them. To Kristine, it seemed they'd never worried about anything. Perhaps in this way, they were true artists.

Kristine and Carter ordered craft beer, she a wheat and he an IPA, and sat in the corner at a high-top table. Kristine half-expected Carter to look at the television, where a basketball team raged across the court, but instead, he focused on her, lifted his beer, and said, "I can't remember the last time I was on a date."

Kristine laughed, completely surprised by his honesty. In New York, it was better to lie about things like that.

"I hope it isn't embarrassing to say that out loud," Carter said, wincing. "I guess I just wanted to say so, in case I'm especially awkward."

Kristine waved a hand, genuinely pleased by his honesty. "I can't remember the last time I was on a date with a good guy."

Carter winced again. "A good guy? Isn't it true that nice guys finish last?"

"I don't believe in rules like that." Kristine smiled, surprised she was having fun.

"You look really nice, by the way." Carter eyed her cardigan and her long boots. He wore a navy blue button-down and a pair of jeans, just as she'd expected he would.

"Thanks. My twin sister is an artist. She helped me pick the outfit," Kristine explained.

Carter was intrigued. "An artist! I didn't know people could become that. Not really."

"She's a pretty special person. I was always so strait-laced while she danced to the beat of her own drum." Kristine sipped her beer. "She has an opening in New York City next week. I'm going back to support her."

Carter's eyes were shadowed for a moment. "Do you think you'll come back to Bar Harbor afterward?" He didn't say it out of a sense of ownership, only curiosity.

"Oh, definitely." Kristine didn't want to get into her breakup or losing her job, as it felt too heavy for a first date. "I've enjoyed the peace and quiet here. Plus, I really want to help my Aunt Kim out as she heals."

Carter brightened. "I think it's amazing you're helping your aunt. All we have is each other. I really believe that."

A server arrived to take their order. Kristine decided on a bean burger with goat cheese, while Carter opted for a beef burger with cheddar and fried onions.

"Fries to share?" Carter asked, passing the menus to the server.

"Oh, yes." Kristine nodded excitedly. "I can't remember the last time I had fries."

"What? Are you insane? I probably have fries once a week." Carter laughed to himself, adding, "My cholesterol is probably not the greatest."

"You work outside with your hands. You can have a few fries here and there."

Carter's eyes opened wider. "So can you. You know why?"

Kristine shook her head.

"Because they're delicious, and life is short." Carter lifted his beer and sipped it, grinning that adorable grin.

Kristine was momentarily jealous of whoever would ultimately fall in love and marry Carter. He would make that woman very happy one day.

Why couldn't it be Kristine? The thought struck her, and she furrowed her brow.

But already, Carter swung easily to other topics, asking

about the city, her hobbies, and her sense of Bar Harbor. Apparently, he'd hung with Hannah, Angie's daughter, a few times and found her "hilarious." "Her baby's really cute, too. Must be terrifying to be a mother so young."

"She's taken it in stride," Kristine said.

"So, Hannah is related to you how?"

"She's my mom's boyfriend's sister's daughter." Kristine counted out the degrees of separation on her hand and laughed. "My family is complicated. It's hard to explain."

"Try me."

Kristine did her best to explain the story of her mother, her grandmother's abandonment, and the fact that her Aunt Nicole and Aunt Casey weren't her aunts at all. Throughout the story, Carter nodded easily, unbothered by the strangeness of the tale. Obviously, he'd been through too much madness of his own to think twice about hers.

"Families, huh?" He laughed.

"You've got that right."

Their burgers and fries arrived. Kristine watched as Carter took a large, juicy bite, so unlike Patrick, who would have used a knife and fork. Kristine followed suit, getting ketchup and mustard all over her fingers. The food was delicious and messy. The laughter swam between them, easy and unquestioned.

Kristine had never had a better first date. Not in her entire life. She even finished her burger rather quickly without asking herself if she should take it in a doggy bag to go. She was hungry, and she allowed herself to eat. This was a revolutionary experience.

After they finished, Carter paid and suggested they head down the road to another bar. Kristine saw no reason to say no. She bounced along next to him as snow fluttered around them, chatting about whatever came to her mind. With Carter, she didn't have to pretend to be anything better than what she was. She'd left her shame in New York City.

Once at the bar, several of Carter's friends walked over to shake her hand. A handsome construction worker named Jeff said, "Carter hasn't been able to shut up about this date."

To this, Carter grunted, "Man? What are you doing? Are you trying to embarrass me?"

Jeff's girlfriend, a woman named Cindy, laughed and said, "Don't listen to them. They fight like children. Carter says you're new to Bar Harbor?"

Kristine nodded and slipped into a stool beside her, conscious of the heat of Carter's body behind her. She longed for him to wrap his arms around her.

"Yes. My mom lives here, and I'm taking some time away from the city," she explained.

Cindy's eyes were difficult to read. "The city is too chaotic for me. All that noise and pollution! And last time we went, we paid thirty dollars for one pizza. One! It wasn't even that big, either."

Kristine laughed. "I don't miss those prices. But you have to admit that the pizza is to die for."

"I prefer Bar Harbor pizza," Cindy said, her eyes shifting toward Carter and Jeff, who laughed joyously. "But that's just me."

The night continued on until midnight, at which time Carter and Kristine walked outside and leaned against the brick wall to gaze at the pregnant moon. Kristine had just called Bella to come to pick her up, as she didn't want Carter to drink and drive. His house, apparently, was just up the road.

"I had a really nice time tonight." Carter tilted his face so that his lips were only a few inches from hers.

Kristine had never ached to kiss someone more. She stepped forward, her heart on her sleeve, and felt Carter's arms around her waist. There was no time for another word. He pressed his lips against hers softly, and her eyes closed with his tenderness. She'd never been handled so lovingly.

Suddenly, a car horn blared. Kristine leaped back, turning to find Bella in the front seat of their mother's car, howling with laughter. Kristine rolled her eyes and caught Carter's gaze again.

"Sorry about that."

Carter looked delirious with love. "I hope we can try again some other time."

Kristine smiled. "Thank you for a beautiful night." She squeezed his hand a final time and whipped into the front seat of her mother's car, her ears filling with Bella's rampant laughter. "Come on, Bella. Grow up," she teased.

Chapter Sixteen

T he next week at the Bar Harbor Airport, Kristine's phone buzzed in the airport security bucket. Bella, busy removing her belt and shoes, lifted her eyes to catch the name across the screen: **CARTER.**

"Aw." Bella wagged her eyebrows as she slid the rest of her items through the scanner.

Kristine's cheeks burned with embarrassment. "He's pretty good at texting. I'll give him that."

"What about kissing?" Bella asked, stepping into the full-body scanner, where she stopped, lifted her arms, and spread her feet apart.

"Good grief."

Kristine followed after her, imitating her. Soon after, they were busy shoving their feet back into their boots and wiggling their laptops back into their backpacks. Around them, other travelers put back on their coats and corralled toddlers, aware that once given a chance at freedom, the toddlers would take it.

"Let's get a cup of coffee," Bella said, adjusting her ponytail before she strung her backpack over her shoulder. "You can tell me more about kissing Carter."

"Bella..." Kristine warned, scampering after her. Their flight was set to leave in a little more than an hour, which gave them enough time for a coffee and a chat. The topic at hand, of course, was Kristine's third date with Carter of the week.

The problem was Kristine wasn't sure how to talk about it. When she was with Carter, she felt head-over-heels for him, quick to laugh and quick to tease. The kissing was transcendent, the kind that made her weak in the knees. During each date, she'd forgotten herself, her body, and her sense of time.

Then again, Carter had never been a part of Kristine's plan. For years, Kristine had made every decision with her career and future in mind. Patrick had fit so beautifully into that mold. Carter, on the other hand, was a tree guy, a part-time mechanic, a part-time construction worker, and, most importantly, the only guardian for his little brother. Why would Kristine, who'd graduated so high in her university business class, settle for a simple life in Bar Harbor with Carter? It didn't make sense.

"Come on. Out with it." Bella sipped her coffee, her eyes narrowed. "There's something going on."

Kristine shrugged, her eyes far down the concourse, where a young couple kissed as though they would never see each other again.

"I can tell you like him. Like, really like him," Bella continued.

"I do." Kristine answered without thought.

"Then why the hesitation?" Bella demanded.

Kristine stuttered, at a loss. "I'm just having fun, Bella."

Bella didn't look convinced. "You've never 'just had fun' your entire life."

"That's mean."

"It's true," Bella returned, not unkindly.

"Maybe I'm learning to have fun," Kristine tried. "Maybe that's part of this trip to Bar Harbor."

"Yeah. You got a job after three days," Bella shot back.

"And I got fired," Kristine returned. "Because I was outside, having fun with you." She stuck out her tongue playfully, trying to get her sister off her back.

"All I'm saying is, Carter seems good for you," Bella continued. "Why won't you give me the juicy details? The kissing? The adorable things he's told you?"

Kristine was surprised at herself for not sharing this with her twin. There was something sacred about the way Carter had cupped both of her hands in his and whispered, "I don't think I've ever met anyone like you before." There was something personal, something she wanted to keep for herself, about the way he'd pressed his lips against her temple and told her he would keep her safe on their snowmobile ride.

Bella and Kristine weren't seated next to each other on the plane, which gave Kristine a break. As other passengers got on the plane and shoved their bags in the overhead compartments, she scanned the internet for news about Patrick and Richard's sexual harassment lawsuits. All she found was the fact that the woman who'd sued them was "having trouble getting interviews in the business world." Kristine closed her eyes. *What kind of world was this? Women had no say in how they were treated.*

Kristine had mentioned the story of the sexual harassment to Carter without telling him her ex was involved. At this, all the blood had drained from Carter's cheeks. "Around here, we're raised to know that women are just about twice as intelligent as men and much more organized." Kristine had laughed through tears at this, marveling at the goodness of this man.

At JFK Airport, Kristine and Bella waited for over an hour before Bella's paintings were released from under the plane. She'd packed them in a massive box with plenty of padding, which had cost an arm and a leg to bring with them. "There they are," Bella breathed, sliding her hand over the cardboard. The rest of the paintings were back at Bella's studio, which they planned to pick up that evening. The next two days would be filled with hanging paintings and preparing the gallery space for the big night. Friends had already hung hundreds of posters to advertise the event, and Bella expected a decent turn-out. She'd even priced some of her paintings in the thousands of dollars— a rate Kristine thought to be overwhelmingly large. She would never understand art.

Kristine had been nervous about returning to New York City. She'd run out of there seeing red, terrified of what the "evil" city would continue to do to her. It had taken her boyfriend and her career; what was next? Once back in Brooklyn again, however, Kristine opened her arms to the city, grateful to see old sights and reconnect with who she'd been before. After they dropped off the paintings at the gallery space, they met friends from college for dim sum and talked about all the gossip they'd missed since they'd retreated to Bar Harbor.

"Everyone is calling Bar Harbor your 'winter retreat,'" their friend, Claire, told them. "It sounds so exotic."

Kristine laughed, but Bella took it seriously.

"I've gotten so much done up there," she said. "I couldn't have finished my art show without it. For a couple of days, I was literally trapped in our house due to a snowstorm, painting myself to death."

Claire blinked, impressed. "You should bring me next time. Maybe I would finally finish my novel."

"Kristine's going back next week," Bella pointed out.

Kristine's cheeks burned with embarrassment. Claire eyed her curiously.

"Still no return for our Kristine?" Claire asked.

Kristine stuttered and sipped her wine. "I'm helping out our aunt. She was in a coma for all of January, and she still can't walk properly or do much around the house."

Claire stiffened. "Aren't there nurses for that?"

"I adore my aunt," Kristine said, suddenly angry at Claire for suggesting it. "We watch old romantic comedies and talk about life. I wouldn't want her to be stuck with someone who doesn't really care about her."

"And Kristine has such a big heart which makes her the perfect caregiver," Bella affirmed, her eyes glowing with love for her sister. "It's hard to believe she belongs to the cut-throat business world."

"Ha." Kristine took another sip of wine.

That night, back in the cozy and very small apartment the twins shared, Kristine collapsed on her bed and read over the texts Carter had sent.

CARTER: Have a great time in the city!

CARTER: Maybe one day, you can show me around.

CARTER: Oh, by the way. We're going to have a little party at my place next week. Cindy and Jeff really want you to come (I think they like you better than me). I hope you can make it!

Kristine's heart burned with a mix of emotions. *A party in Bar Harbor?* That probably meant drinking domestic beers, eating chili, and playing cards. It wasn't that she was against those kinds of parties; it was just a very different scene than her usual one.

Wasn't she supposed to be in New York City, eating dim sum, going to gallery shows, and dating men with big dreams?

Out in the living room, Bella greeted Florian excitedly. "You brought wine!"

Kristine fell back on her pillow, her heart aching. The feelings she had for Carter were impossible to ignore. But why couldn't she have what her sister had? Bella and Floridan were artists and city people. That was supposed to be Kristine's world, too.

Kristine began to text a reply to Carter, but soon deleted it. She felt inarticulate and sleepy. She would text him in the morning, maybe send him a picture of a bagel or a Brooklyn street. He wanted the best for her; he genuinely adored her. Maybe she could find a way to give in.

On the afternoon before Bella's art show, Heather and Luke met Kristine, Bella, and Florian at a little Mexican restaurant a few blocks south of the gallery space. Kristine, Bella, and Heather were dressed immaculately, each in tall boots, their long black hair shining. Like always, they lined up against a red brick wall and had their pictures taken with Heather in the middle. People passing by stopped to say, "Wow. You look like triplets!" All three laughed, grateful for the compliment that they'd heard a thousand times before.

Florian was very charming. He made Heather laugh and teased Bella lightly, his arm around her waist. Luke was impressed with him and asked him a number of questions about his life in New York City. All the while, Kristine felt strange and out of place, crunching tortilla chips and looking out the window. A masochistic part of her wanted Patrick to walk by, maybe with a girl beside him. She wanted to learn how to dislike him even more.

Bella's paintings hung around the well-lit gallery space, illustrating Bella's chaotic creativity and clear sense of self. Kristine and Heather walked from painting to painting, commenting on each quietly as other New York art-people stepped around them, looking at price tags. Several feet away,

Bella was in her element, chatting up art journalists and giving answers that sounded both intelligent and humble at the same time. Florian watched her, beaming with pride.

"She's really something," Kristine said to her mother. There was a clear edge of jealousy to her voice.

"She is." Heather's eyes flashed. "But so are you."

"Tonight isn't about me," Kristine pointed out as she moved to the next painting, which looked a lot like a blob fighting a triangle.

"No, but another night will be." Heather squeezed Kristine's upper arm. "How has it been to be back?"

"It's been fun," Kristine answered. "Maybe even too much fun. I can't help but think I'm missing out on something."

Heather nodded. "Nobody is keeping you in Bar Harbor, you know."

"I need to be there for Kim."

"Jennifer and I can handle that."

Kristine furrowed her brow. "What I mean is, I want to be there for Kim. I think the time together has been good for both of us. Good for me, anyway."

Kristine couldn't admit how wonderful it was to be needed in a concrete way. Kim needed help around the house, to clean her bathroom, to cook her dinner, and the get into bed. Kristine was grateful to feel necessary. It filled up her heart to the brim.

"Just keep tabs on yourself and what you really want," Heather breathed.

Kristine wanted to laugh. *How could anyone really know what they wanted?* Instead, she said, "Thank you, Mom," and she wrapped her arms around Heather, willing herself not to cry.

A bit later, a text came through from Carter. Kristine had written him that morning, unsure if she'd wanted to.

CARTER: Hey! I know you're busy. Just let me know when you're back in town. :)

Kristine's heart dropped into her stomach. When she lifted her eyes, she found a handsome and familiar face in the crowd. It was Roger, a guy she'd known back in business school. She waved him down, and he hugged her, saying, "Wow! I thought you'd skipped town."

"I couldn't miss Bella's big night."

"Of course." Roger sipped his wine and smiled wider. "I heard you got out of Richard's clutches just in time."

Kristine wrinkled her nose. "He wasn't exactly the greatest boss."

"No. I wouldn't think so. Brilliant man, though."

Kristine's heart hardened. What about a sexual harasser and all-around bully was "brilliant" exactly?

"What are you up to?" Kristine asked him instead.

Roger told her he'd just been promoted in his company, that he was making six figures and thinking about renting a new apartment in Greenwich Village. The conversation made Kristine feel three inches tall. When he added that he and his girlfriend had just gotten engaged on the Greek island of Santorini, she nearly shattered the wine glass in her hand.

"That's such great news," she heard herself say, concentrating hard on keeping it together. "I'm so happy for you both."

Chapter Seventeen

I t was difficult to leave Bella in New York City. Kristine held her twin tight, her throat so constricted that she hardly managed to say, "I love you." Bella knew how troubled Kristine was. She squeezed Kristine's shoulders and said, "Don't push yourself to do anything you don't want to do." This confused Kristine even more.

Back in Bar Harbor, Kristine texted Carter she'd returned. She stood in her pajama pants and a pair of thick socks, a glass of wine in her hand as yet another snowfall floated down outside. Carter texted back immediately to ask if she wanted to grab a beer and tell him about her trip.

KRISTINE: I'm super tired. Maybe we can try another time this week?

Carter was so understanding. This hurt Kristine even more. Why was she pushing away this very handsome, kind man? What was wrong with her?

Abby and Hannah entered the kitchen, Hannah with her baby wrapped so that she hung gently but securely on her chest. They chatted about their budding photography business and their upcoming "action-packed wedding season." It was hard for anyone to believe that spring was right around the corner. March was only a couple of days away.

"How was New York?" Hannah asked, her hand cupping her daughter's head.

"It was amazing," Kristine lied. "Bella killed it at her show. She sold almost all of her paintings and was written up in several magazines and newspapers."

"Our girl is well on her way!" Abby cheered.

Kristine smiled and excused herself, allowing Hannah and Abby the kitchen for their meeting. The baby whimpered gently for a moment, but Hannah soon calmed her, her voice gentle and sweet.

The next day, Kristine arrived at Kim's place around noon. Jennifer breezed out the door with frenetic energy, clearly grateful to have some time out of the house. She barely asked Kristine about her trip to the city and instead said, "There's plenty of ingredients in the fridge. Try not to let her have too much sugar."

Kristine waved as Jennifer slid into her car and reversed out of the driveway. She then stepped into the warmth of the foyer and latched the door closed behind her.

"Is that who I hope it is?" Kim called from the kitchen.

Kristine laughed, her heart lifting for the first time in days. She entered to find Kim vibrant looking, her hair billowing down her back. When Kristine complimented her, Kim said, "Jennifer finally took me to have my hair done. My roots were despicable."

"They weren't that bad," Kristine insisted.

Kim arched her brow. "There's no reason a woman shouldn't look her best. Even in the darkest of times."

Jennifer had left several dishes in the sink. Kristine turned on the radio, grateful for something to do with herself and her anxious mind, and began to scrub them. Kim chatted easily about the previous few days, including what she'd watched on television and the little snacks Robbie had brought over. Kristine had a hunch that Kim's insistence on fixing her hair had everything to do with her budding romance with Robbie.

"Oh, and Kristine!" Kim brightened. "I took three steps at the silly physical therapy session the other day!"

Kristine turned the water off, jumped around, and exclaimed, "No way!"

"Relax, honey. I didn't win an Olympic medal or anything." Still, Kim was clearly pleased with herself.

"It's the first part of the process. I know that." Kristine waved a hand. "But you'll be right as rain in just a few months. I'm so proud of you."

There was a knock at the door. Kristine raced to answer it, excited to see Robbie again. There he was, burly but nervous as a teenage boy in love. He held a bouquet of lilies, baby's breath, and little purple blossoms Kristine couldn't identify.

"Hi, Robbie!" Kristine opened the door so he could enter. He stomped the snow from his boots and said, "There she is. Our city girl is back home."

Kristine blushed and watched as Robbie walked toward the kitchen, clearly overwhelmed with love. Kim's voice was like a song. "Oh. Robbie. What did you do?" To this, he said, "I just thought you deserved something nice to look at. Plus, you walked three steps! That's something to celebrate!"

Kim's laughter echoed through the kitchen. "Everyone acts like I walked on the moon."

Kristine joined them in the kitchen, pouring them both cups of coffee and telling Robbie bits and pieces of her trip to New York. Robbie was only half-impressed, but soon found time to ask the question on his mind.

"And how is it going with Carter?" Robbie's eyes shone with intrigue.

A stone lodged itself in the base of Kristine's stomach.

Somehow, she managed to keep her smile up. "Oh. He's pretty good. I haven't seen him since I got back."

"He's just about the greatest young man I know," Robbie said with a firm nod. "He hasn't dated much over the years."

"Too many responsibilities," Kim affirmed.

"But I always knew he would find someone to change his mind." Robbie beamed.

Kristine blinked several times. She hadn't texted Carter back that morning. *Was it better to call him that night and tell him it was over? Was it better to break the connection before it got too thick?*

"He's really lovely," Kristine agreed. "We've had a lot of fun."

Suddenly, the mug in Kim's hand fell to the ground and shattered into hundreds of pieces. Coffee spilled across the hardwood, cutting between the floorboards. Kristine froze with shock, then looked at Kim. Her head was tilted strangely, and her eyes had rolled into the back of her head, showing nothing but white.

"Kim! Kim!" Robbie leaped to his feet, all the blood draining from his face. Then, Kim began to shake, her feet pounding on the ground. Robbie pressed on her shoulders, trying to stabilize her.

Kristine leaped for her phone, terrified. "Make sure she doesn't bite her tongue!" she cried as she dialed 9-1-1.

Robbie seemed helpless. As Kim's seizure continued, he flailed around, searching for something to help. Finally, he managed to slip a thin book between Kim's teeth, which kept them from her tongue.

"What is your emergency?" A hard-edged woman on the other line demanded.

Kristine spoke quickly, explaining that her aunt was having a seizure, which was probably a side-effect of a serious brain injury. She requested an ambulance as soon as possible.

By the time Kristine got off the phone, Kim's seizure had subsided. Her eyes had closed with exhaustion, and she was slumped forward, her forehead on Robbie's shoulder. Robbie's eyes were filled with tears. Tenderly, he placed his hand over her hair and stroked her head, whispering that everything would be all right.

Kristine filled a glass with water and knelt to speak. "Try to drink some water, Aunt Kim. Please."

But Kim shook her head against Robbie's shoulder, too tired to do anything but be held. Kristine was terrified, still shocked at the severity of the seizure. Outside, sirens blared, coming for them. She rushed for the front door, which she held open for three EMT workers— two of whom carried the gurney.

"No, Robbie. I don't want to go to the hospital. Not again." In the kitchen, Kim's voice was urgent and filled with sorrow. "Please, Robbie. I don't want to go."

Kristine hustled back to the kitchen. There, Robbie bent to kiss Kim's forehead and whispered, "We have to make sure you're all right, Kim. Please, let these kind men take you where it's safe."

Kim closed her eyes tightly. Sweat had formed across her forehead.

"Please, Kim. Do this for me," Robbie breathed.

Very slowly, Kim nodded. The EMT workers lowered the gurney to the height of her wheelchair so they could easily shift her exhausted body onto it. There, she held Robbie's hand, her eyes searching his.

"We'll meet you at the hospital, Kim," Robbie told her firmly. "We'll be right behind you."

"Family can go in the ambulance," one of the workers said as they wheeled her toward the door.

Kristine leaped back, suddenly focused. "I'm family," she said, grabbing her coat from the front closet. "I'm right behind you."

Kristine had never been in an ambulance before. It was alienating, filled with machines and gadgets— things meant to break people open and sew them back up again. Kristine sat beside Kim's gurney and held her hand as they breezed toward Bar Harbor Hospital. She wanted Kim to know how much she loved her, how much she needed her to get well again.

"I feel so foolish," Kim muttered, her eyes opened only slightly.

"Why would you ever feel foolish?" Kristine asked, trying to lighten her voice.

"Shaking around like that," Kim whispered. "I must have looked like a maniac."

"Kimberly," Kristine warned. "You have nothing to feel foolish about. Just relax. Think about what you want to do when you get out of the hospital. We'll make chocolate sundaes with maraschino cherries and whipped cream. We'll watch another romantic comedy— maybe something with Jude Law?"

Kim furrowed her brow. "He's just too blond."

Kristine laughed, surprised at how painful it felt to feel so joyful and so frightened at once. "Okay. Okay. We'll find someone else."

"Gerard Butler, maybe," Kim mumbled. "I like that accent."

"We'll make it happen," Kristine promised.

Kristine closed her eyes and said a small prayer. Kim's grip was tight around her hand, proof of just how alive she truly was.

Once at the hospital, the EMT workers wheeled Kim into the back, leaving Kristine in the front with a clipboard and a million fears and questions. She sat in the chair with a pen poised above the paper she was meant to fill out, listening to the chaos of a half-full emergency room. Babies cried. Accident survivors pressed bandages over open wounds. Kristine felt heavy with dread.

Suddenly, Robbie breezed through the door, his eyes searching. When he spotted Kristine, he rushed to the seat next to her, where he collapsed and shook with sorrow. "How is she? Gosh, I was terrified. Terrified!"

Kristine squeezed his arm. "She seems okay. I promise you. They just took her back. The doctor will tell us what's going on soon."

Robbie pressed his hand over his chest. His reaction was palpably dramatic, proof that he'd lost so many people and had grown accustomed to very bad news.

Kristine stood to buy them bottles of water and called Jennifer, who didn't take the news well. Kristine could hear it in Jennifer's voice: She almost felt as though Jennifer was pointing the finger at Kristine for the seizure happening, but Kristine knew deep down that Jennifer didn't mean to insinuate anything. It was coming from a place of fear.

"She's already at the hospital?" Jennifer demanded. "Did you make her ride in the ambulance alone?"

"Of course not," Kristine breathed, trying her best not to match Jennifer's anger. "She seems a lot better."

"I'll be there in ten," Jennifer blared, then hung up the phone.

Back in the seating area, Robbie drank his entire bottle of water in thirty seconds and gasped for air. Kristine's heart thudded with sorrow as she watched the doors open and close, open and close, waiting for Jennifer. She prayed they would all be home soon, safe in the warmth of their homes.

Chapter Eighteen

Kim was in and out of consciousness that evening. Sometimes, she felt herself being moved from room to room, the wheels under her hospital bed squeaking. Other times, she awoke long enough to have a brief conversation with the doctor or a nurse. Around seven-thirty, a platter of very disgusting hospital food was brought to her, along with the news that she had visitors.

Jennifer shot into the room first, like the bullet of a loaded gun. She looked stricken with her hair wild around her face. "Mom!" She rushed to Kim's side and hugged her, shaking slightly with surprise and sorrow. "How are you feeling?"

Kim wanted to laugh off the seizure. She really did. But in truth, the entire thing had terrified her. She'd felt somewhere outside of her body, knowing it was out of her control. The pain had throttled along her jawline and her shoulders. It had seemed to last hours, days. And then, she'd come-to with her head against Robbie's shoulders as Robbie had sobbed.

But instead of telling Jennifer how frightened she was, Kim lied and said, "I feel right as rain, honey. Really."

Jennifer pulled her head back and looked Kim in the eye. So often, it frightened Kim how much her daughter looked like her. Life came in cycles.

"You promise you feel okay?" Jennifer asked.

Kim nodded. "The doctor wants to put me on another silly medication. I'll find a way to choke it down."

Jennifer rolled her eyes, accustomed to her mother's playfulness. She then collapsed in a plastic chair beside the bed and eyed her mother's plate of food. "I see the food here hasn't gotten much better since last time."

Kim laughed and prodded what looked like a sirloin steak with her plastic fork. "Can we order burgers?"

Jennifer rubbed her eyes and smeared her makeup. "Kristine and Heather are waiting to see you. And the neighbor, Robbie."

Kim's heart lifted. Sheepishly, she said, "I can't believe he waited around all that time."

Jennifer raised an eyebrow. "Mom. What is going on with Robbie?"

Since Robbie's return to Bar Harbor, he'd kept tabs on the schedule at Kim's place and more-or-less aligned his visits with Kristine and Heather's time there. Both Heather and Kristine were easier, eager to sit back, laugh, and listen to Robbie and Kim's stories. Jennifer, on the other hand, liked to nag Kim, demanding that she focus on her health and wellness more often. Jennifer made very little small talk with Robbie, who often felt like a fish out of water while Jennifer was around. This made Kim very sad, as she felt it meant her daughter didn't want her to have real, everlasting happiness.

Before Kim could answer, Kristine, Heather, and Robbie entered the hospital room. Robbie held another bouquet of flowers, completely different from the ones he'd brought her only that afternoon. These were red roses.

"There she is! Our drama queen!" Kristine joked as she

walked around the side of the bed and kissed Kim on the cheek.

"You know me. I need the world to revolve around me." Kim laughed.

Heather kissed Kim on the cheek and stepped aside so that Robbie could take Kim's hand in his and say, "You gave me quite a scare today, missy."

Kim's cheeks were hot. "You didn't have to buy me more flowers, you know." Not for the first time, she imagined what it would be like to kiss Robbie on the lips. *Was she too old for something as frivolous as a first kiss? Did she believe that you could ever be too old for anything?*

"This wasn't some dramatic ruse to get me to buy you more flowers?" Robbie teased.

Kim laughed again, her eyes closing. Around her, Heather, Kristine, Jennifer, and Robbie sat, as though she was a big show they'd paid to see. Still, her heart went out to each of them. How had she gotten so lucky to have so much love in her life?

The next afternoon, the doctor cleared Kim to go home. Kim was surprised, as she'd assumed she'd be trapped in the hospital for another month, maybe two. That was just the course of things, she'd thought.

Jennifer bustled around the room, preparing for Kim's departure. She spoke about the healthy meal she planned to cook that evening, about the early bedtime she wanted Kim to take on, and about all the other changes she wanted to implement, if only to make Kim's life "ultimately healthy" and, to Kim, very boring. *What was the point of living, anyway?*

"Did you just say 'kale salad' to my face?" Kim asked, half-joking.

Jennifer paused, her bag hanging from the crook of her arm. "What do you mean?"

"I've never purposefully eaten a kale salad for dinner in my life," Kim said.

Jennifer's face was stony. "I think we need to focus on your nutrition. Make sure you're getting all the vitamins you need."

"And I think I'm doing just fine," Kim returned. "I eat a balanced diet. To me, that includes a bit of sugar here and there. A bit of butter, too."

Jennifer sighed. She sat on the edge of the plastic chair, depleted. "I just want you to be well."

Suddenly, Robbie, Kristine, and Heather arrived for visiting hours. Jennifer eyed them angrily, not wanting anyone else to get in the way of her plans.

"Good news. I'm busting out of here," Kim announced.

Robbie punched the air. "That's fantastic!"

"I'm so happy for you," Heather said, her eyes welling up.

Kristine did a happy jig. "I guess it's about time for that Gerard Butler romantic comedy. Oh, and the chocolate sundae."

"What are you talking about?" Kim asked, laughing.

Kristine waved a hand. "Oh. Nothing."

"I do think Gerard Butler is fantastic. That accent is to die for!" Kim said.

Kristine's eyes twinkled knowingly. Robbie blushed, embarrassed. Kim reached for his hand, which he took gently into his. She imagined a beautiful future where she and Robbie could hold hands like this every day, no matter the circumstances. A walk down the beach. A sunset. Dinner at an Italian restaurant.

"Take me home, Robbie," Kim heard herself say.

Jennifer's jaw dropped with surprise. Her eyes cut from Kim to Robbie and back again. "Oh, it's okay, Rob. I can take her."

But Robbie shook his head. "The lady has spoken. I'll make sure she gets home safe."

"I have a plan for tonight," Jennifer insisted. "And there's so much to worry about, between the wheelchair and the medication and all that. I can take her."

Robbie eyed Jennifer, looking fearful.

"Robbie knows all about the wheelchair and the medication," Kristine said, stepping forward. "You've been a great help at Kim's place. Not that Kim ever needs any help. Not really."

Kim laughed and stuck out her tongue. "Don't tease me."

Jennifer bristled. "If you really think you can handle it."

"He's a grown man, Jen. I think he can handle this little old lady just fine," Kim said.

Finally, Jennifer acquiesced. She collected her things and watched helplessly as Robbie helped Kim into her wheelchair, where she settled easily. "It fits like an old glove," she tried to joke, although she did hate that wheelchair more than anything in her life.

Robbie wheeled her out of the hospital, through the white-washed hallways and past other patients who weren't as lucky as Kim. Kim knew she shouldn't have walked away from such a severe brain injury. Good luck had never followed her, not like this.

At Robbie's truck, he lifted her swiftly into the front passenger seat, broke down the wheelchair, and put it safely in the back. Kim waved down at Jennifer, Kristine, and Heather, feeling like a teenage girl headed off to prom. Kristine passed up the flowers from her hospital room, which Kim placed on her lap. The scents were intoxicating.

"You'll call us if you need anything?" Kristine called through the window.

"You'll be the first to know when I need that chocolate sundae and Gerard Butler!"

Robbie laughed and buckled his seatbelt in the driver's seat.

Kim was suddenly flushed, aware that this was one of the first times she'd ever been really and truly alone with this handsome man. As Robbie's truck was older, it had gears, and he shifted the stick from PARK with a trained hand. The way he drove reminded Kim of her father, so long ago, taking her and Melanie off to gymnastics. Her heart ached with missing him.

For a little while, Kim and Robbie drove without speaking. The silence was pleasant, especially after the heinous beeping and cries at the hospital. Kim had thought several times that she never wanted to die in a hospital if she could help it. After these recent stints, she felt even more sure of herself.

"Thank you for coming up to the hospital when it happened." Kim heard herself speak.

The truck was stopped at a red light. Robbie raised his hand and wrapped it over hers so that her heart rammed against her ribcage. *Why did his touch feel so intoxicating?*

"I genuinely don't know where else I could have been. Last night, I stayed up late just thinking about you. About how much I don't want to lose you."

Kim sighed. This was what she'd been afraid of.

"I know you've lost so many people," she breathed. "Maybe, with my declining health, we shouldn't..." She trailed off, unsure if she wanted to say this. "I just don't want you to get hurt again."

Robbie flashed her a look of warning. After a long pause, the light turned green, and he had to take his hand back to change gears. He drove quietly, his eyes focused, until he suddenly turned right toward the Acadia Mountains. This was the opposite direction from Kim's place.

"Where are you taking us?" Kim asked softly.

"Let's go for a drive," he said. "Unless you don't feel up for it?"

Kim's eyes widened. "After being cooped up in the hospital, it's everything I want in the world."

Both Kim and Robbie had been born in Bar Harbor, beneath the Acadia Mountains and alongside the churning blue of Frenchman Bay. To them, it was the most heavenly place in the world, lined with huge, stoic pine trees, ancient rocks, and miles and miles of hiking trails. Kim's heart ached with the memory of hundreds of hikes, many of which she'd taken with her ex-husband. She prayed for a future of hiking with Robbie by her side. She prayed for Christmases, Thanks-givings, and Fourth of Julys.

Slowly, Robbie snaked the truck through the mountains, weaving through the rocks to find better views of Frenchman Bay and the mighty horizon of the Atlantic Ocean. Kim felt breathless and finally said, "I can't believe it's real."

Robbie's smile was crooked and endearing. He stopped the truck at an overlook, cut the engine, and dropped his head back. Together, they took in the splendor of the middle of the after-noon. A sharp wind rushed against the windshield and shook the bed of the truck.

"You scared me yesterday," Robbie finally said, his voice low. "Terrified me, in fact."

Kim tried to speak, to tell him again that was why she thought they should cut their romance short, but Robbie inter-rupted her.

"It made me understand how much I care for you," Robbie said. "And how I can't just cut those feelings out. Why would I?" He turned to lock Kim's eyes with his. "Why would we stop feeling this? To avoid pain? Kim, haven't we both been through enough pain to know that pain is inevitable? I'd rather choose life, beauty, and love, rather than safety. Wouldn't you? Wait. Don't answer that." He shook his head, resolute. "I know you. I know the way the Kim I know would answer."

Overwhelmed, Kim leaned toward him, needing his lips upon hers, his hands on her body. When he kissed her, she no longer felt like the broken hospital patient she'd been only hours before. She felt young, free, and alive— making the choice to keep her heart open to the possibility of a possibility.

When their kiss broke, Kim was surprised to learn she'd been crying. She dropped back on the seat, mopping herself up. "Look at me. I'm such a schmuck."

Robbie laughed and handed her a clean handkerchief. People didn't keep handkerchiefs on them like they used to. The fact that Robbie did, pleased her to no end.

That night, Robbie set Kim up in front of the television, poured her a glass of non-alcoholic wine, cracked open a beer, and put on a film. The movie was called *On Golden Pond*, and it featured Katharine Hepburn and Henry Fonda, who lived on a beautiful pond but had multiple family dramas and difficulties. The reflection of real life was palpable.

After the film, Kim sipped the non-alcoholic wine and said, "How strangely difficult it is to be a person. Huh?"

Robbie laughed kindly and kissed her hand. "It's the hardest thing I know."

That night, Robbie helped Kim prepare for bed. When she was too exhausted, he took over the toothbrushing, helped her wash her face, and even helped her change into pajamas. He slipped her easily beneath the covers, then teased her and said, "Want me to read you a bedtime story?"

Kim shooed him away, her heart in her throat. It was too early for a real sleepover; she'd told him that herself earlier that evening. Still, she was grateful that he would be just next door, in the guest bedroom.

She had a hunch that he wouldn't be in the guest bedroom for long. Perhaps in a month, maybe two, she'd invite him over. Perhaps then, she'd allow herself to acknowledge the true depths of her feelings. If she didn't allow herself to fall in love again, then what was the point of life?

Chapter Nineteen

Since Kim's seizure, Kristine had felt listless and out of touch with her own reality. The look in Kim's eyes when she'd fallen into the seizure terrified her. One minute, Kim had been there— laughing, making jokes, and falling in love with Robbie, and the next, she'd been someplace else. It was a reminder of the preciousness of life, Kristine knew. But it also told her a story of how much she had to lose.

Several days after the seizure, Kristine was wrapped up in a blanket on the couch at the Keating House. Heather was off on a date with Luke; Bella was living out her wildest dreams in New York; and the rest of the Keating-Harvey clan was spread across Bar Harbor, making the most of themselves. The next day, Kristine would be back at Kim's for only a couple of hours, as Jennifer was paranoid about Kristine's inability to care for Kim properly. The seizure had happened on her watch, after all.

Despite her packed schedule, Bella seemed in-tune with Kristine's feelings. She texted now, heavy with regret for not being there.

BELLA: You should do something tonight. Have you seen Carter lately?

Kristine groaned, shoving her phone between the cushions of the couch. Confusion about Carter, Kim's health, and her place in the world had left her frozen. As hours drifted past, however, she found herself coming back to the same conclusions.

One: that she didn't want to spend another hour of her life in a corporate environment. And two: that Carter was just about the best chance she had for romance. Why was she so afraid of saying yes to happiness?

Kristine retrieved her phone from the cushions and texted him back.

KRISTINE: Hey. Long time, no speak. Sorry about that.

KRISTINE: It's been a hectic week. I don't know if you heard, but my Great Aunt Kim was in the hospital again.

Kristine stared at her text messages. They seemed to make poor attempts to right the wrong of bad communication. Suddenly, overwhelmed with the desire to make things right again, she decided to call him. It was the only way.

The phone rang three times before Carter's familiar voice came through the speaker.

"Hello." He sounded tired and reserved. There was no flirtation to his voice at all.

"Hi. Carter?" By contrast, Kristine sounded like an excited little girl. "It's Kristine."

"Yeah. I know." There was silence.

Kristine sat up straight, her feet on the floor. "Hey. I'm really sorry it's taken me so long to reach out since I got back from New York. There's really no excuse."

Carter sighed. "It's okay. I mean, it has to be okay."

Kristine's heart lifted. "Would you like to meet for a drink tonight? I have so much to tell you. And I want to hear how your week has been, as well."

Carter sounded stiff. "I don't know, Kristine. I've had a really long day."

"Just one drink," Kristine urged. "I promise I'll make it worth your while."

Again, silence. In the background, music played. Kristine realized that she'd never seen his place before. Maybe she never would.

"Listen, Kristine. I'm sorry about your aunt. I really am." He sounded like a stranger. "But I hardly heard from you over the past week. I may not have dated much, but I'm not an idiot. I know what the silence means."

Kristine stuttered. Why had she thought he would sit around, waiting for her?

"I really can explain," Kristine told him timidly, unsure if she believed herself.

"Take care, Kristine," Carter said firmly. "It was really nice to get to know you for a while. I wish you well, whether you stay here in Bar Harbor or head back to the city."

Kristine had a frog in her throat. "You take care, too."

After that came the click. Carter had hung up.

Kristine sat and stared into space for a good ten minutes. This was yet another blow in a series of terrible blows— yet this one, she knew, she'd caused herself.

Too blue to hang around at home for long, Kristine put on her winter boots, wrapped herself up in Kim's winter coat, and stepped out into the blistering cold. There was something refreshing about it, something that made her feel nourished, alive. She locked the door and hustled for the road, where she could see the soft orange glow of just-lit streetlamps in downtown Bar Harbor. The walk was no more than twenty minutes, and Kristine needed every bit of it. As her legs stretched out and her head cleared, she tried to tell herself a story of the rest of her life. It came up blank.

Downtown, Kristine walked for a while, past the candy store, which was still decorated for Valentine's Day, past several of Evan Snow's restaurants, and past the post office and library. At the corner, she paused for a moment, watching a red pickup truck drive by. A part of her prayed she would stumble into Carter. Another prayed not to experience his anger in person.

The sound of music came from down the block. There was the banging of drums and the vibrato of a saxophone. She was led toward it like a ship to a siren and soon found herself in the second row of tables at a tiny jazz club. Luke's sister, Angie, sat at her piano, twinkling through a solo, as her boyfriend, the handsome drummer Paul, paraded across the snare and bass with studied ease. The other musicians, a saxophonist, a trumpeter, a trombonist, and a bass player, cut through the jazz tune, improvising when it was their time to shine. At the end of the song, Kristine shot to her feet with applause. She was surprised to learn she'd begun to cry.

A waiter came to take her drink order. "A glass of wine," Kristine whispered, returning to her seat with embarrassment. "Thank you."

With her glass of wine in front of her, Kristine allowed herself to fall completely into the dream of Angie's jazz ensemble. Toward the end of the set, she lifted her phone and texted Bella back.

KRISTINE: I messed things up with Carter. He's made it clear he doesn't want anything to do with me.

BELLA: Oh no! Oh, Kristine. I'm so sorry. Maybe he'll come around.

KRISTINE: I don't know if I deserve it. He's a great person.

BELLA: So are you.

KRISTINE: I think I'm more lost than good right now. It isn't fair to him.

BELLA: :(

BELLA: I love you, sis.

KRISTINE: I love you, too.

After the jazz ensemble finished for the night, Angie stepped around her piano, bowed alongside her other band members, and made a beeline for Kristine. Kristine stood and hugged her, closing her eyes as she said, "I can't believe how talented you are."

Angie laughed. "And I can't believe you're here! I was so surprised when I peered out and saw you in the audience."

The waiter hurried over with a glass of wine for Angie, winking as she placed it on the table. "Your usual, Miss Angie."

Angie thanked her and sat, crossing one leg over the other. Another jazz ensemble stepped on stage, preparing to dive into the next set. "They're pretty good," Angie whispered. "Especially the saxophonist."

Kristine nodded, grateful to fall into someone else's world for a little while.

When the music started, Angie glanced toward Kristine and asked, "How has it been for you, living in Bar Harbor the past month?"

Kristine wrinkled her nose. "I wish I could give a happy answer."

"I can understand that. After Chicago, this place wasn't easy for me. On top of that, Hannah and I had to start all over again. New jobs. New friends. Thank goodness for your mother for welcoming us into your family. Then again, we couldn't rely on her for everything."

Kristine nodded, remembering that Angie had left Chicago after a divorce. On top of that, she'd learned that her parents had adopted her and that her mother had abandoned her and Luke at a very young age. It had been a whirlwind of epic proportion, much worse than anything Kristine had gone through the past month.

Still, she couldn't compare. Pain was pain.

"I just keep wondering, when am I going to feel all right again?" Kristine asked, her voice breaking.

Angie's eyes caught the light from the stage. "You have to believe you will. Even in the darkest moments."

Kristine dropped her gaze and sipped her wine. It sounded so simple.

Paul appeared at the table and planted a kiss on Angie's cheek. "Paul, do you remember Kristine? Heather's daughter?"

"Of course!" Paul greeted Kristine warmly. "How did we sound?"

"You were incredible," Kristine said, trying to smile. "I feel very lucky that I caught so much of the set."

Paul blushed. "I'm grateful every day that Angie formed that little jazz ensemble. I don't know where my life would have gone without it." He eyed Angie lovingly. "She had the bravery to start something new while I was more-or-less content to sit around my living room for the rest of my life."

A bit later, Kristine excused herself to go to the bathroom. There, she splashed her face with water and took stock of herself, of her still-youthful twenty-three-year-old face, and of the messiness of her outfit, which was nothing she would have stepped outside wearing in New York. Nobody seemed to care.

Paul's words continued to echo in her mind. "The bravery to start something new." Kristine could understand the instinct to hang around in a living room forever, watching TV. But it wasn't how she wanted her life to go.

When she stepped out of the bathroom, Kristine found herself face-to-face with a community bulletin board. There, people posted pamphlets and fliers which advertised: "Babysitter: $10 per hour," "Servers Wanted at the Rusty Bucket," or "Guitar Lessons Available." Other signs offered rooms for rent in apartments and houses, used cars, and even animals for sale.

One pamphlet, in particular, caught Kristine's eye.

Nursing School at the College of the Atlantic

"Nursing is one of the fine arts: I had almost said 'the finest of the finest.'" — Florence Nightingale, the very first "modern nurse."

"Every nurse was drawn to nursing because of a desire to care, to serve, or to help." — Christina Reist-Heilmeier, RN.

Beneath the quotes was a write-up about the College of the Atlantic, which was located in Bar Harbor and welcomed only a few hundred students per year. According to the flier, the classes were small, allowing for a more hands-on approach in the field of nursing.

Kristine tugged the flier from the wall, suddenly over-whelmed. Back in business school, she'd been driven to become a money-crazed lunatic. *Why?* There was nothing behind that journey but more money and more arrogant men.

When Kristine got back to the table, she paid for her drink and wished Paul and Angie a beautiful night. She then hurried back to the Keating House, where she sat at her computer and sent a very serious email to the dean of the nursing sector of the College of the Atlantic, citing her recent work with her aunt, her understanding that the business world wasn't for her, and her drive to care for those in need. She typed furiously, without error, and soon sent the email off, feeling as though she'd just taken the first step toward something she really, truly wanted.

Heather and Luke returned from their date, both brimming with smiles and smelling like freshly fallen snow. Kristine leaped from the couch to hug her mother, buzzing with promise.

"How was your date?" she asked them.

"Aren't you a sight for sore eyes," Heather said, taken aback at Kristine's good mood.

Kristine shrugged, grateful for the secret of her new plan. It gave her power. "I'm just happy to be here, is all."

Heather rubbed Kristine's shoulders. In the kitchen, Luke popped open a bottle of wine and asked if anyone wanted a glass. Kristine followed her mother into the kitchen, watching as Heather and Luke kissed and talked about the wine, its regions, and its grape varietals. Their lives had changed over and over again, transforming into this newfound, beautiful story. Kristine had to have the strength to change, too.

Chapter Twenty

Three Weeks Later

Professor McLear had worked in the field of nursing for thirty years before her decision to become a teacher. To Kristine, she was sharp as a whip, clear and concise, and eager to bring more nurses into the fold. "Nursing is my passion," she explained to the class on the first day. "But it's not for everyone. Remember that every moment of every day, you have the privilege to change your mind. If, at any point, you have second thoughts about nursing, come talk with me. Maybe I can calm your fears— or maybe I can point you in a different direction. It's my job as your professor to guide you, and I never want to lead you astray."

Kristine had never hung around much with students in the medical field. In the classroom, she studied them— their clothing, the way they spoke to each other. As it was midway through the semester, most everyone knew everyone else, and

Kristine felt like the "new girl." This pleased her. It meant she had a fresh slate.

On the first day, Professor McLear leaped directly into scientific materials. She passed out pamphlets about the circulatory system, the digestive system, and the lymphatic system, explaining that there would be a test in three weeks.

"As this is a half-semester class, it's important that we jump directly into the material," she explained. "We only have nine weeks to learn as much as we can."

* * *

Kristine had been accepted into the College of the Atlantic a week after she'd submitted her application. That week of waiting had been grueling. She'd spent a great deal of it wandering through the Acadia Mountains, chatting with Kim about her innermost fears, and experimenting with new recipes in the Acadia Eatery with Nicole and Luke. More and more, New York City felt like a distant memory. Bella's dispatches from there were strange, about "crazy" parties with other artists and "insane" prices for hot dogs and soups. When she'd received confirmation that she'd been accepted to college, she'd shrieked with joy. "A nurse," Heather had breathed. "It fits you so well, my darling. I can't believe I've never seen it before."

After the first class with Professor McLear, Kristine zipped up her spring coat and headed outside. March sunlight warmed her cheeks, and the snow had melted, leaving mushy mud beneath brown grass. Other students milled about, heading to their next classes or the food court. As there were limited half-semester classes available, Kristine had managed to sign up for only three classes— nine credits total. "It's not a bad start," her new advisor had told her. "You can make up for lost time over the summers and graduate in two and a half years if you work for it." To this, Kristine had said, "I'm ready to work for it."

Kristine stopped at the food court for a cup of coffee and a croissant. She sat in the corner, watching people and eavesdropping. She'd been frightened that she'd feel "too old" compared to the other students and was now pleased that the students ranged from eighteen to thirties. She was either smack-dab in the middle or somewhere on the younger side. "People go back to school all the time," her advisor had said. "This is an admirable thing."

The men in the food court were handsome, athletic, and quick to laugh. Kristine eyed them curiously, a part of her imagining meeting someone on campus, settling down here in Maine. Still, she mourned her brief relationship with Carter. The three dates they'd been on had been magical. She'd felt like a better, happier person.

Kim had suggested over coffee that Kristine contact him again. *"I mean, come on, Kristine. You're a beautiful woman. He knows that."* To this, Kristine had said, *"I was very cruel to him. There's no making up for that."*

As she drank her coffee, Kristine texted Kim with a report of her first day.

KRISTINE: My first professor was super tough but fascinating. I took eight pages of notes, and my hand is killing me!

KRISTINE: How was physical therapy today?

Kim wrote back a few seconds later.

KIM: I'm glad your first class went well!

KIM: Physical therapy was just fine. Robbie says I'll be running the marathon in no time. I think he's disappointed that I won't need the wheelchair by summertime. What good will he be to me then? :)

Kristine laughed aloud. Several people in the cafeteria eyed her curiously. The romance between Robbie and Kim was so endearing, so heart-filling, that she couldn't wipe the smile from her face. *Who knew you could find such new happiness at the age of seventy?*

Two classes later, Kristine packed up her backpack and headed for the bus stop. Heather had almost insisted that Kristine take her car for the day, but Kristine had wanted to take the bus. She didn't have her own money for her own car yet— and she wanted to focus her efforts on building her own life without too much of her mother's help. "The bus works for so many other people, Mom. Besides, I can use the travel time to study."

When Kristine opened the front door of the Keating House, a shriek reverberated through the windowpanes. Bella rushed down the staircase, her black hair flailing behind her. She wrapped her arms around Kristine, crying out about how cold she was. Then, she kissed her on the cheek and exclaimed, "There she is! My college student!"

Kristine blushed and limped through the door, burdened by her twin. "What are you doing here?"

"I came here to celebrate your big day!" Bella cried.

Kristine was genuinely pleased. A part of her had thought Bella would move on without her into her city world of artistry and fine dining. Instead, Bella's face was wide-open with curiosity.

"You have to tell me everything. Every person you talked to. Everything your professors said," Bella insisted. "All I do every day is paint myself to death. My head is losing knowledge! You need to restore it!"

Kristine laughed. She removed her coat and hung it in the front closet as Heather stepped out of the kitchen with a big bowl of cookie dough in her arms. "I was thinking about your first day of school almost twenty years ago. When you got home, you, Bella, and I made cookies together, and the two of you told me about your days."

"Aw," Bella cried. "That's so sweet."

"I thought we could recreate the memory," Heather said. She tilted the bowl toward them, urging them to take a little sliver of unbaked cookie dough. It was obviously the greatest delicacy in the world.

Bella grabbed the big wooden spoon, scooped a large morsel of cookie dough from the bowl, and ate a decent chunk of it, her eyes closing.

"Bella!" Heather laughed. "Make sure we have some to bake."

Kristine doubled over with giggles. "I swear, not much has changed in twenty years. I bet you did the same exact thing after our first day of kindergarten."

"Guilty as charged," Bella quipped.

With delicate hands, Heather rolled cookie dough into balls and baked the cookies while Bella and Kristine sat at the kitchen counter, catching up. Bella poured them glasses of a natural wine she'd brought from a wine shop in the city and chatted about another painting she'd sold that week.

"Oh. I meant to tell you." Bella paused, nervous. "I found someone interested in paying your half of the rent. Just for a few months."

The outer edges of Kristine's heart crackled. Was she really okay with someone moving into her bedroom in the city and taking up residence of her old life? Then again, she was now a student at the College of the Atlantic— with many more years ahead of her.

"I think that's great," Kristine heard herself say. "There's no reason someone shouldn't take my room."

Bella's smile was slightly sad. "You're really out of the city for good, aren't you?"

Kristine and Bella had never spent so much time apart. Kristine wondered if, slowly, over time, they would lose track of each other. Perhaps their "twin link" had been dependent on their close quarters the past twenty-three years rather than some mystical thing.

"Anyway," Bella said quickly, shaking her head. "I'm so proud of you. I wasn't lying when I said you take wonderful care of people. The business world is so tragic and pathetic. Oh! That reminds me." Bella's eyes glittered with intrigue.

"Oh no. Tell me this isn't about Patrick," Kristine said.

Heather spun around. "Do not say that terrible man's name in this house!"

Kristine laughed. "Don't worry, Mom. He isn't the bogeyman."

"It's about Patrick. And he very well could be the bogeyman." Bella wrapped her hair into a coil and whispered, "Anyway, I guess the woman who accused him and your boss of sexual harassment has a bit more power in the world than initially thought. Her father is a big-time reporter at the *San Francisco Tribune*. The Tribune has been writing 'think pieces' about the difficulties for women in the business world and using your ex-boss and your ex-boyfriend as bad examples. *The New York Times* has picked up several of the articles."

Kristine's lips parted with surprise. She'd largely been avoiding the internet and the news, focusing solely on her commitment to nursing school.

"Anyway, I heard the woman who accused Richard and Patrick of sexual harassment already got a better job doing business financials for a prestigious art magazine," Bella continued. "Meanwhile, I heard that Patrick's new girlfriend dumped him, Richard has fired him, and he's bumming around Brooklyn bars, spending too much money, and flirting with whoever is around. It's generally pathetic."

Kristine was flabbergasted. She'd never have envisioned this future for the All-American over-achiever, Patrick.

"Finally, the bad guys finish last," Kristine said.

"I'd say that's something to celebrate," Heather affirmed.

After the cookies came out of the oven, Kristine, Heather, and Bella each ate one (moaning at the sea salt and gooey dark chocolate), packed up twenty in a container, dressed in coats and hats, and headed for the Keating Inn. There, Heather tracked down Luke for a hello kiss, and Kristine and Bella passed cookies around to Abby, Nicole, and other staff members. A maid who bustled past gasped and said, "Oh gosh. I haven't had time to eat in hours! Thank you!" She then hurried away, exclaiming at how yummy the cookie was.

"Let's go downtown," Heather said as she stepped out from the Acadia Eatery kitchen, her lipstick smeared from kissing.

"Mom." Bella pointed at her own lips and winked. "You're like a teenager in love."

Heather blushed and hunted for the mirror in her purse. Through the small window of the swinging kitchen door, Kristine could make out Luke chopping away at a cutting board, whistling loudly. Their love was overwhelming.

Downtown, Heather, Kristine, and Bella sat in a little wine bar with a bay window that looked out on the frigid waters of Frenchman Bay. Candles flickered cozily on tabletops, and people bowed their heads to speak in low, conspiratorial tones. Often, laughter punctuated the air. It was very much a place for gossip, for juicy conversations with the people you loved most.

Heather ordered a bottle for the table, along with hummus, cheese dip, soft pretzels, and fresh vegetables. As Bella talked about Florian, Kristine lay her head on Bella's shoulder and felt the vibration of her voice. Her sister was clearly in love.

"You should bring him to Bar Harbor when it's warmer!" Heather said. "He'd love it here. You two could just make art and go sailing, hiking, and swimming all summer long."

Bella's eyes widened. "Everyone wants to get out of the city for the summer."

"And you have a safe haven here. With us," Kristine said, popping up from her shoulder.

"Will you be around this summer? Or will you be off saving lives already?" Bella asked.

"I don't think they'll throw me into a hospital any time soon," Kristine said with a laugh.

"I'm assuming your life will be just like *Grey's Anatomy*," Bella offered. "Complete with hunky doctors."

Kristine blushed. Again, she thought of Carter for no reason at all— the way he'd smiled so eagerly when she'd told a story and the way he'd so capably driven the snowmobile, her arms wrapped around him for safety. She hadn't seen him at all since their very brief romance had ended. Robbie never brought him up, even though Kristine ached for him too.

"I still can't help but think I really messed things up with Carter," Kristine heard herself admit, surprising herself with her honesty.

Bella's shoulders dropped. "This is what our twenties are about, I think. We make mistakes. We have regrets. But we keep going."

Heather nodded and wrapped her hand around Kristine's. "If it's meant to be, he'll find his way back to you."

Kristine's heart lifted at the possibility, even as Bella shook her head and reminded her, "But there will be so, so many hunky doctors in your future. Remember that."

Chapter Twenty-One

"Uh oh." Heather glanced at her phone as they gathered their things from the wine bar, preparing to leave. "Your Aunt Nicole just sent me a grocery list a mile long."

"That's a classic Aunt Nicole move," Bella joked.

"She works her tail off at the Eatery, always making up new recipes. I think she's on another creative kick right now. She says she plans to 'experiment' tomorrow." Heather continued to read the grocery list as they walked toward the front door. "How in the world does she plan to use a grapefruit? Truffle oil? Sardines? I cannot wait to find out."

Heather drove the three of them to the grocery store a few blocks away, where they parked and headed into the chaos. It was a Monday evening, and the aisles were filled to the brim with shoppers, mostly mothers who stuffed their grocery carts with cereal boxes and packages of pasta. Heather said hello to several as they passed by, one hand lifted as the other wielded the cart.

Kristine and Bella had gone grocery shopping with their

mother thousands of times. In the old days, it had been up to them to convince Heather to buy whatever junk food they'd craved— pop tarts, Twizzlers, and sugar-packed lemonade had been favorites. Now, they helped Heather load the cart with kale, red onions, broccoli, sweet potatoes, and a thousand other Nicole-approved items, chatting easily and waiting their turn to get into packed aisles.

The wine section was located near the cash registers, with a good view of the exit doors. There, the three of them paused to assess the French wine regions and discuss what would pair best with the very strange list of ingredients Nicole had sent. Heather knew more about wine than Kristine and Bella put together and had made it a mission to fill in their wine knowledge a little bit at a time.

As Heather lifted a Bordeaux from the shelf, three wiry teenage boys in big hoodies whipped down the alcohol aisle. Two of them had filled their arms with bags of chips, candy, and pop tarts, while the third had four bottles of vodka and a twenty-four pack of domestic beer. Their eyes were alive and mischievous. It was already clear they had no plans to pay.

The three teenage boys bolted past Heather, Kristine, and Bella and headed for the door, giggling madly. They very nearly reached the parking lot when suddenly, a guard stepped between them and the doors. One of the kids tried to dart around him, but the guard smacked a button that locked the doors immediately. The three kids staggered back, still clinging to their "goods" for dear life.

"Oh my gosh," Bella whispered, her hand around Kristine's arm.

"What in God's name do the three of you think you're doing?" the guard demanded, loud enough for everyone in the store to hear.

One of the teenagers tittered, overwhelmed with the drama.

"Please. I'd love to know just what you thought, trying to steal alcohol as minors?" the guard continued to blare.

Kristine stepped forward, abandoning her mother and Bella to get a better look at the teenagers. Just as she'd suspected, the tallest of the three boys had dirty blonde hair and bright blue eyes, just like Carter. Even the shape of his nose was similar.

These were the same boys who had stolen from her at the candy shop. One of them was TJ, Carter's brother. And yet again, they'd been caught breaking the law. Kristine's heart went out to Carter, who spent his whole life trying to protect this silly, aimless teenage boy.

Suddenly, in the midst of the guard's speech to the teenagers, Kristine bolted up beside them, gasped for air, and said, "Oh, TJ! I've been looking all over the store for you."

Carter's little brother, TJ, froze with surprise. He smiled, confused, his eyes flashing.

Kristine pointed at the items in the boys' arms. "Thank you for collecting everything for me. I wouldn't have been able to find all that stuff myself."

The guard gaped at her. "You wouldn't have been able to find chips, candy, and vodka by yourself, ma'am?"

Kristine nodded. "I get overwhelmed in big stores like this. TJ has been such a big help." She looked him directly in the eye and said, "I really don't know what I would have done without him. Here, why don't you put your stuff over at cash register three? I can pay for it right away." Kristine smiled sweetly at the guard, praying her little stunt would work.

The guard rubbed his fingers through his thinning hair. He looked from Kristine to the boys and back to Kristine, then asked, "Were you three gathering these groceries for this nice woman?"

Slowly, the three boys nodded, clearly at a loss. *Why had this crazy lady come to save their hind ends? Was there a catch?*

"This way," Kristine instructed before she lost her nerve.

She led the three teenagers back to cash register three, where Heather and Bella met her. Heather wore a confused smile, but Bella nodded knowingly. She'd put the puzzle pieces together.

The three teenage boys watched, non-phased, as their vodka, chips, candy, and beer were raked over the scanner. After that, the woman at the cash register scanned the rest of Nicole's list— the broccoli, the kale, and the very fancy cheeses. Combined, it was the strangest grocery order in the world.

As Heather, Kristine, and Bella stepped into the parking lot, the boys walked behind them, hanging their heads like bad dogs. Before they could run away, Kristine turned on a heel and glared at TJ, her anger spiking.

"TJ Bilson," Kristine blared. "Were you really going to throw away your future over a few Cheetos and a pack of beer?"

TJ skulked. "Who are you, anyway?"

"It doesn't matter who I am," Kristine shot back. "What matters is this. Your brother does everything for you. He sacrifices his own life and happiness to put you through school and make sure you have a bed to sleep in. Is this behavior how you repay him? What if he had to leave an important job today just to pick you up at the police station? What if he lost hard-earned money just because of your stupidity?"

TJ's jaw dropped with shame. He continued to stare at Kristine, as though she was a ghost who'd walked out of the wall.

"Tell me you won't put your brother through this anymore," Kristine demanded, her nostrils flared. She then turned to stare at both of TJ's friends, whose cheeks were bright red. "Tell me you'll think twice before you do something this stupid."

TJ sputtered. "Okay. Fine. Yeah." He swallowed. "I promise."

As the three teenagers limped away, nursing their wounds, Kristine, Bella, and Heather loaded up the car with groceries.

Heather whistled, impressed, before she asked, "So, I take it that was Carter's younger brother?"

Kristine nodded, her eyes glistening. "It really makes me angry that TJ treats Carter with such little respect."

Heather closed the trunk door and snapped her hands together. Bella had nabbed a bag of candy from the boys' stash and carried it with her to the back seat, where she tore it open and nibbled at the edge of a gummy. Kristine grabbed herself one while Heather beckoned from the front for her own piece. Together, the three of them sat in the heated car and snacked, all heavy with their own thoughts.

"Do you think this will get back to Carter?" Bella asked.

Kristine shrugged. "I guess not. I don't know why TJ would tell Carter about this."

"It's too bad," Bella breathed. "What you did for Carter is really romantic."

Heather nodded, her eyes locking with Kristine's in the rear-view mirror. "Maybe some of the most romantic things in the world always remain secrets."

Chapter Twenty-Two

W ith Bella home, a family party was planned for later that week. "Finally, another reason to celebrate!" Aunt Casey had joked as Nicole had written out yet another list of groceries. The house was warm and alive, with people coming and going and Bella's laughter ricocheting from wall to wall. For brief moments, Kristine was able to forget the dark parts of the year— and remind herself that it was still only March. There was still so much to live for.

Kristine worked diligently toward Friday, taking the bus to campus, writing pages of notes, and keeping herself focused on her goals. She made small talk with other students on campus, asked questions of her professors, and even watched a few *Grey's Anatomy* episodes with Bella, which Bella called "research."

Friday late afternoon, a few hours before the family party was set to begin, Kristine and Bella decorated the Keating House with candles, streamers, and big bouquets of flowers. With Nicole, they'd created a menu that matched the hilarity of their grocery cart several days before. There was broccoli with spicy seasoning, beef tartare, fancy quesadillas, and Spanish croquettes— plus a selection of vodka drinks and multi-colored jello shots inspired by the boys and their hope for a wild, rebellious teenage party. Plus, Kristine and Bella put out all the chips and candy the boys had tried to steal, laughing excitedly about the story.

It was no surprise that Kim and Robbie were the first guests to arrive. Kim was always eager for a party and had been cooped up at her house long enough. Easily, Robbie carried her up the porch steps as Kristine brought her wheelchair up behind her. "I always feel like a princess, too lazy to use my own two legs," Kim joked.

"I'll carry you wherever you want to go, Your Highness," Robbie joked as he settled her back in the wheelchair, adjusting her hair over the back of the seat. His movements were so tender and careful that you would have thought he'd been helping Kim in her chair all this time.

"The house looks fantastic!" Kim cried. "And it smells delicious. Goodness. You've outdone yourselves, as usual." She smiled wide, looking beautiful and effervescent. She'd done her makeup and had experimented with a new eyeliner technique, one normally used by younger women. It suited her. She was the sort of woman willing to try anything.

"And Bella? Tell me. How is the city?" Kim said, wheeling herself into the kitchen.

"It's all right," Bella said. "I have to admit, I've missed having my sidekick around."

"Sidekick? Is that really how you think of me?" Kristine laughed, following Kim into the kitchen, where she took a piece of candy from the bowl.

"What a varied selection of foods." Kim looked quizzical. "I know you love junk food, but it's getting out of hand."

"I have to admit that I'm not one for fine dining. This looks spectacular to me," Robbie said, taking a chip.

Kim chuckled and locked eyes with Kristine. She sensed something was up.

"The story of the weird snacks is hilarious," Bella explained quickly. She reached behind her to collect two red jello shots, which she passed to Robbie and Kim. "These teenage boys at the grocery store tried to steal all this vodka, beer, and junk food. The guard was about to destroy them for stealing, but Kristine stepped in like a hero and saved the day."

"Kristine!" Kim's lips formed a round O. It didn't take long for her to put the pieces together. "I don't suppose one of those teenagers was TJ Bilson?"

"Oh. Yeah. I mean, I wasn't sure at first, but one of them looked so much like Carter. I couldn't just stand by and watch him get into even more trouble." Kristine stumbled over her words.

Robbie's face was stoic. He took another chip, chewed it slowly, and said, "That TJ has broken Carter's heart over and over again."

Kristine's cheeks burned with embarrassment. "TJ is probably just a confused teenager like we all were."

Robbie eyed Kim, his expression full of something Kristine didn't fully understand.

"Well, TJ has great taste in beer, vodka, and snacks," Bella tried to joke. "I haven't had a jello shot in years. Shall we?"

Kim placed hers back on the table, saying, "I'm still abstaining. That's good news for all of you, though. More jello shots to go around."

"Oh, great." Robbie laughed sarcastically and loosened the jello shot from the shot glass.

"Someone's done this before." Bella clinked her glass with Robbie's. "Bottom's up!"

Aunt Nicole breezed into the kitchen, bringing with her a wave of beautiful perfume. She inspected the food on the stovetop and chatted easily with Kim and Robbie, discussing the new recipes at the Acadia Eatery and a recent write-up a journalist had done about the Keating Inn.

"We're already fully booked for half of the summer," Nicole explained. "And it's only March!"

"That's ridiculous," Robbie said. "I remember when this place was hungry to fill even half of its rooms."

"That was before the Harvey Sisters came to Bar Harbor like a storm," Kim said.

That night, the dining room table was filled to the brim with beautiful food placed on fine china. The Harvey-Keating-Talbot clan gathered around, squeezing themselves around a table that shouldn't have been able to handle that much love. Kristine grabbed the chair beside Kim's wheelchair, squeezing Kim's hand as the others adjusted around them. Across from her, Bella laughed at a joke Abby had said, showing off lips stained with wine. A few seats away, Luke kissed Heather's cheek adoringly, and beside him, Paul and Angie whispered in one another's ear. Aunt Casey and Uncle Grant squabbled over who would sit next to their daughter, Melody, who was visiting from the city, while Nicole loosened Evan Snow's tie, which he'd worn to the house after a grueling afternoon of business meetings. Out the window was a beautiful view of Aunt Casey's newly constructed house, just another segment of the ever-widening world of the Harvey Sisters.

Kristine was so grateful to be a part of it.

"How are those New Year's Resolutions going?" Luke joked, his glass of wine raised as the table quieted.

"I think it's safe to say I'm not very close to my goals," Hannah said with a laugh. "But being a new mother means keeping my head above water, and that's about it."

"Well said. Here's a toast: to keeping our heads above

water, and knowing that sometimes, that's all we can do," Heather said, raising her glass.

Hannah smiled, eyeing her mother sheepishly. Kristine's heart went out to each of them— their chosen family members, who were the leftovers from so many terrible decisions made by so many people who were now dead. If Kristine's grandmother, Melanie, hadn't decided to bail on motherhood, Heather never would have been raised with Nicole and Casey, and Kristine and Bella wouldn't have had them in their lives at all. Maybe they'd have eventually met their Great Aunt Kim; then again, Kim and Melanie had never really gotten along.

Everything had happened the way it was meant to.

"You've outdone yourself yet again," Evan Snow said to Nicole, his eyebrows raised as he loaded his fork with more beef. "I've been so well-fed since I met you, Nicole Harvey."

"They say it's the best way to a man's heart," Heather joked. "But it was reversed for Luke and I. I can barely mash a potato." She ate a piece of broccoli, her smile wide.

"That's a lie," Luke said. "I'm sure you could mash a potato. I just wouldn't trust you to get it quite right." He stuck out his tongue playfully as Heather shrieked.

After plates were scraped clean and big serving dishes began to show their bottoms, Kristine stood to take things back to the kitchen. The table was almost overwhelming, with gossip and laughter bouncing from one corner to another. She needed a few minutes by herself to breathe.

At the sink, Kristine rinsed the dishes and began to line them in the dishwasher, listening to the sounds of her massive family in the next room. It occurred to her that in the future, her nursing career would help patients enjoy many more nights like these with their own family members. Her heart filled with happiness at the thought.

"You're hard at work in here." Kim's voice came through

the doorway. She'd wheeled herself in, her lap piled with more dirty dishes and sticky forks and spoons.

"You didn't have to do that!" Kristine laughed and collected the dishes from Kim.

"Why not? I'm a perfect transportation device," Kim joked. "Here. Why don't you rinse the plates, and I'll line them in the dishwasher."

"You really don't have to."

Kim furrowed her brow. "Don't make me insist again."

"All right. All right." Kristine laughed, grateful for Kim's company. One after another, she rinsed the plates and passed them to Kim, who lined them up expertly.

"It sounds strange, but I've really missed being able to do menial housework," Kim explained. "Robbie hardly lets me lift a finger. Lucky for me, he's a darn good cook and cleaner. His first wife must have had a wonderful life with him, a husband who actually helps around the house. Of course, I've read on the internet that those dynamics have changed quite a bit. Younger men do more housework. They love to cook."

Kristine blushed. "It would be wonderful to find a man like that. I like scrubbing toilets just as much as the next woman."

Kim laughed. A moment later, however, her smile fell off her face. Worried something was wrong, Kristine shut off the water from the faucet and asked, "Are you okay?"

Kim nodded, still serious. "I need you to know I told Robbie not to contact him. It's not our business what happens between the two of you."

Kristine cocked her head. "What are you talking about?"

Kim nodded toward the bowls of chips and pop tarts. "Robbie's a big softie. It's part of the reason I'm falling in love with him. You saving TJ Bilson from the guard at the grocery store really riled him up."

Kristine's heart dropped into her stomach. "Oh no, Kim. You're not saying what I think you're saying, are you?"

Kim wrinkled her nose. "As I said. I told him not to."

Kristine grabbed her phone from her pocket, suddenly terrified. Only one person had texted her, though, and it was a friend from New York— not Carter.

"Do you know what Carter said when Robbie told him?" Kristine asked softly.

Kim shook her head. "Robbie didn't say."

Kristine tugged at her hair, suddenly anxious. "I don't want him to think I did that just to get his attention."

Kim placed her hand on Kristine's. "Don't pull your hair out, honey. What matters most is you care about that young man. He should know how much you care. Don't you think?"

Kristine's lower lip bounced. "I treated him terribly, Kim. I really did. I don't deserve his attention or his kindness."

Kim lifted one shoulder. "We're all unkind sometimes, Kristine. What matters most is how we apologize."

Suddenly, there was a knock at the front door. Kristine's stomach knotted.

"Who could that be?" Heather asked the table. "Did we invite someone else tonight?"

"I'll get it!" Bella called, always eager to make the biggest waves.

"Oh no. Oh no." Kristine spoke under her breath, terrified.

Bella whisked toward the foyer. Next came the sound of the big front door opening, along with Bella's cry, "Oh goodness. What are you doing here?"

Kristine's eyes widened. "Kim? I don't know what to do?" She was full-on panicking now.

Suddenly, Robbie walked into the kitchen, his face very pale. "Kristine, Kim told me not to do it. I'm so sorry. I always meddle in other people's business. It's my worst trait."

"Hi. I'm sorry to drop by like this." Carter's voice came through the house. Immediately, it sent electricity up and down Kristine's spine and filled her heart with promise.

"I really am sorry, Kristine," Robbie whispered as he placed his hands over Kim's shoulders. "But sometimes, I think young people wait too long to live their lives!"

Kim rolled her eyes and laughed. Kristine dried her hands on a kitchen towel and stepped toward the foyer, where she stood and gazed at Carter in the doorway, all bundled up, his shoulders lined with a late March snow. His blue eyes shone with intrigue and something else— fear, maybe.

"Hi." Kristine sounded timid, like a child.

Bella gesticulated wildly. "Why don't you come inside for a little while? We have plenty of food and wine and coffee and jello shots."

Carter cocked his head. "Jello shots?" Nevertheless, he stepped through the door and stomped the snow from his boots. His eyes continued to lock with Kristine's, as though he didn't want to let them go. Not again.

Suddenly, Robbie appeared on the other side of Kristine, his hand lifted. "Hi, Carter!" He spoke too loudly, as though he wanted to pretend everything about this was normal.

"Robbie," Carter said, his smile crooked. "You didn't mention there was a family party tonight."

Robbie laughed and eyed Heather and the others at the dining room table. "I hope you don't mind that I invited Carter over. He's been a real help to Kim and I over the past few weeks. He's not just a handyman— he's a friend."

Heather's sapphire eyes were like a lighthouse. Kristine could feel them targeting her from across two rooms. Heather had never seen Carter up close— yet here he was, at Kristine's doorstep, like a hero in a romance novel.

Suddenly, Kristine stepped forward and said softly, "Do you want to come into the kitchen with me?" She had to get Carter away from the prying eyes of all these family members, each so curious about who he was and why he'd come so late at night.

Carter nodded sheepishly. He raised a hand toward the dinner table and said, "I'll just be a minute."

"Nonsense!" Aunt Nicole called. "I'll be insulted if you don't eat at least three plates of food."

Kristine tugged Carter into the kitchen, giving both Robbie and Kim a dark look as they passed by, exiting the room.

"I'm so sorry about that." Kristine felt so flustered and spoke too quickly. "I had no idea Robbie was going to contact you. Now, you're at the mercy of a thousand family members, which is nothing you deserve. Especially after everything that happened."

Carter nodded and removed his winter hat so that his curls whipped in all directions. "I think Robbie set up this trap, and I fell right into it."

"He's a crafty one."

In the next room, the dining family had begun to speak louder and louder, giving Kristine and Carter a safe and quiet space to talk. Nobody could eavesdrop.

"Then again, when it comes to you, I was always willing to fall into a trap like this," Carter added, his voice very quiet.

Kristine's mouth was terribly dry. She closed her eyes, unsure if she should believe him. "Carter, I'm so sorry about how flaky I was. I was the worst kind of woman to date. You were open and ready for whatever this is, and I rejected it. I've regretted it ever since."

Carter's eyes widened with surprise. "I have to admit that I never imagined you'd actually say that. I hoped you would. But I thought you'd surely go back to the city soon and pick back up where you left off."

Kristine sighed. In the silence, she poured them each a glass of wine. As she passed the glass to Carter, she said, "There's no going back for me. It's been a hard thing to admit to myself. But this past week, I started a new career path, one that will keep me in Bar Harbor for the foreseeable future. It's insanity, isn't it? But I guess the most insane part of it is that I actually want this life."

Outside, the house lights glittered against the falling snow. In the distance, Frenchman Bay glowed from the nearby lighthouse and the little houses that lined the coast. Carter followed Kristine's line of sight.

"Then again, who wouldn't want this life?" Kristine said with a smile. "It's the most beautiful one I've ever found."

Carter stepped closer to her, his eyes again locking with hers. Kristine's heart banged against her ribcage.

After another dramatic pause, Carter whispered, "I can't believe you stood up for my brother like that. As soon as Robbie called me about it, I sat TJ down and asked him about the story. After a bit of prodding, he confirmed everything. He also told me that it was the most embarrassing moment of his life." Carter laughed, his eyes closing. "You've done something I've never managed to do. You've embarrassed him into thinking maybe stealing isn't as cool as he once thought."

"I guess that means I'm really an adult now that I can embarrass a teenager," Kristine said.

Carter tugged at his curls. The air between them sizzled with electricity, with promise. "I can't thank you enough. Another arrest would have destroyed him. It would have destroyed me, too."

Kristine nodded. His lips were no more than a few inches from hers. In the next room, Aunt Casey howled with laughter at something Uncle Grant had said, and Bella was insisting that Abby and Hannah come to New York to take street photography. "You wouldn't believe some of the people I see on any given street. Hundreds of people pass you every single day, each with a different story."

"You're really staying here?" Carter asked softly.

Kristine nodded and bit her lip. In time, she would tell him about how much the city destroyed her, about Patrick and her belief that she would never be good enough for anyone and anything.

But just now, the look in Carter's eyes told her that she was good enough— for love, for life, and for new chapters.

Carter placed his hand over Kristine's cheek. Kristine hadn't been touched so tenderly since the last time he'd done that. She was reminded of the way Robbie had carried Kim up the front steps and placed her delicately in her wheelchair. Carter was the kind of man who would be there, in every way, until the very end.

He was the kind of man you clung to for the rest of your life.

"Listen. I know I really messed up," Kristine whispered. "But would you maybe like to grab a drink sometime? We could talk about everything without my entire family one room away."

Carter's smile was enormous. Instead of answering with words, he pressed his lips against hers. Kristine's knees nearly collapsed beneath her. His arms wrapped around her, holding her upright. It was just as beautiful as their very first kiss, yet even more comforting. It was like coming home.

When the kiss broke, something caught Kristine's eye. She lifted her gaze to catch Bella sneaking past the doorway, giving Kristine a silly smile. She'd seen the kiss; she knew the depths of Kristine's happiness in her bones. Maybe they would never lose that twin connection after all. Maybe it would link them forever until they were little old ladies with silver hair, laughing the days away in rocking chairs. Perhaps they would live together in the Keating House— a family home they would never give up, no matter what.

Chapter Twenty-Three

The feeling of spring came all at once. Friday night at the family party had been crisp and snow-filled, but by Monday morning, fifty-degree temperatures felt balmy and freeing, and sunshine erupted from the kitchen window in Kim's kitchen, making the very clean countertops and tables glow.

Jennifer had just stopped by on her way to a doctor's appointment, bringing with her a box of fresh donuts filled with cream. She'd had a pep to her step, proof that the doldrums of winter were now deep in the past. Kim had to appreciate how difficult it had been for Jennifer, sitting day after day at Kim's side during the coma. Now, with Robbie, Kristine, and Heather to help around the house— and Kim's greater grip on health, Jennifer had been allowed to take control of her life back. She was taking exercise classes and considering dating again. As a mother, it was remarkable to see.

Kim now sat in her wheelchair with a mug of coffee, watching the sunlight play across Frenchman Bay. Robbie had just returned from a run and now took a shower in the bathroom. The sound of the water was comforting to Kim, as it seemed so ordinary. She and Robbie now lived so many of their days side-by-side, performing easy tasks. It was remarkable to her that they'd both spent so many years alone, just down the road from one another. *What had taken them so long?*

When Robbie had told his daughter the news of his new romance with Kim, she'd initially taken it badly. "I wanted you to move to Florida. To be near me," she'd begged. But only hours later, Robbie's daughter called back to apologize. "I was being a total idiot. You deserve every happiness. And besides, it's just like you always say. You're a man from Maine. You can't really be anything else."

The walker Kim had gotten from the physical therapist was placed within arm's reach of the wheelchair. So far, she'd only braved walking with the thing when Robbie was around, as her legs remained rather weak. Still, there was something so nourishing about the sunshine on her cheeks, something that told her she could do anything.

With her hands on the grips of the walker, Kim focused, placed her feet flat on the floor, and slowly lifted herself to standing. Gosh, it felt delicious to stand. Her perspective on the world around her shifted. She was reminded of her past self, the woman who'd raced the men on her snowmobile and nearly defeated each and every one of them.

Remaining focused, Kim practiced her walk across the kitchen. Her legs quivered slightly, but she kept going, grateful to perform this everyday action alone.

Suddenly, the doorbell rang. "Come in!" Kim called, knowing her voice would reach the front stoop through the opened windows.

Kristine's voice was like a song. "Hello! I hope you don't mind we decided to stop by!"

Kim's heart lifted. "I'm in here!"

Kristine rushed through the kitchen doorway, her arms

burdened with flowers. When she saw Kim upright, walking very slowly across the floor, she shrieked with surprise.

"Aunt Kim! Oh my gosh!" She placed the flowers on the table next to the donuts, clearly overwhelmed.

"I'm just walking," Kim tried to joke. "I've done it a million times before."

Carter Bilson stepped into the kitchen beside Kristine, placing his arm around Kristine's waist. He smiled, impressed and sheepish at once.

Truthfully, Kim was very proud that she'd managed to walk so far alone. More than that, she was grateful that she'd had an audience if only so she could prove to everyone else just how capable she was and would always be.

"But are you here alone? I thought I saw Robbie's truck," Kristine said.

"Did I hear my name?" Robbie called from the back hall-way. In a moment, he appeared, scrubbed clean, his hair wet and sticking up. He spotted Kim upright on her trek across the kitchen and leaped forward to help.

"Don't you dare," Kim insisted. "I've got this handled."

Robbie laughed. "I should have known you wouldn't need me for long." He then turned toward Carter and Kristine and said, "What are you two up to?"

Kristine's smile was ridiculously happy. If Kim had to guess, Kristine and Carter probably hadn't spent much time apart since Friday night, when Robbie had roped the two lovers together once more with his craftiness. Kim loved Robbie all the more for that. He was right— young people so often waited too long for their lives to begin.

"We just wanted to swing by to say hello," Kristine explained.

"And to thank you," Carter said.

Robbie waved a hand, as though it was no big deal. "Why

don't you stay for dinner? I'm going to cook something special tonight to celebrate."

"Oh, there's nothing to celebrate," Kim said, making her way back to the wheelchair.

"There's always something to celebrate," Robbie corrected her.

"I can help," Carter said. "I've been meaning to show off my cooking chops for Kristine. All we've done all weekend is eat out."

"I didn't know you could cook!" Kristine smiled and locked eyes with Kim, remembering their conversation.

"Of course I can. I'm the guardian of a very hungry teenage boy." Carter rapped his knuckles on the counter. "Who, by the way, has really taken to Kristine."

Kristine blushed. As Kim sat back in her wheelchair, exhausted from just ten minutes of walking, she asked, "So there's no bad blood between you and TJ, Kristine?"

"He seems to be cool with it," Kristine said. "I think he knows he owes me."

"I think it's more than that. He's got a bit of a crush," Carter teased.

"Oh, stop it. He does not." Kristine looked very pleased and dropped her head on Carter's shoulder.

The contrast between Kristine and Carter's relationship and Kristine and Patrick's relationship was palpable. Kim remembered how miserable poor Kristine had been all those months ago, hoping to build a life for herself that just wasn't sustainable.

Kristine and Kim sat at the kitchen table, watching as Carter and Robbie set to work on dinner. Carter showed Robbie his technique to slice garlic with more finesse and precision, while Robbie explained that he put red wine in "just about everything" because he liked what it did to the final taste.

"Isn't this funny?" Kim said quietly as the men busied themselves with another cooking task. "Only a few months ago, we were sitting around here, feeling lonely and watching romcoms. Now, we're living out our own romantic stories."

Kristine blushed and glanced back at Carter, who listened intently to another instruction from Robbie.

"Carter says he thinks of Robbie as sort of a grandfather figure," she whispered, careful not to let Carter hear.

Kim's heart lifted. She couldn't wait to tell Robbie this news later, although she had a hunch it would make him cry. Robbie was very in touch with his feelings, a rarity in men of his age. Kim had hit the jackpot.

Chapter Twenty-Four

Later that week, after another full day of classes, Kristine loaded up her backpack and stepped into the warm, early spring night. Around her, the College of the Atlantic campus was coming to life— the grass greening, the trees beginning to blossom, and she caught herself skipping here and there, as though youthfulness was a state of mind rather than a given truth. She supposed that was something Kim had discovered a long time ago.

That evening, only steps from the bus stop, a truck in the corner of the College of the Atlantic parking lot caught her eye. Kristine stopped and caught sight of two very similar-looking young men seated with their legs hanging from the back of the truck. One of them studied a textbook, while the other read a novel.

It was TJ and Carter.

Kristine practically leaped toward them, overwhelmed with excitement. Halfway across the parking lot, TJ raised his head from his textbook and nudged Carter, who lifted his head from his novel and smiled.

"What are you two doing here?" Kristine asked, trying to catch her breath.

Carter gestured around the beautiful campus. "TJ wanted to see what a real college looked like."

"And what do you think, TJ?"

TJ contemplated the question. His eyes danced across the ornate buildings and big, beautiful trees. "It's definitely not as lame as I thought."

Kristine laughed. "College is just about the least lame thing I know. I like it so much that I'm doing it for a second time."

As he considered Kristine's words, TJ's blue eyes were bright with promise. This version of him was entirely different from the one Kristine had encountered in the grocery store. He'd gotten a haircut and donned a button-down shirt. More than that, there was a cleanness to him, one that suggested he spent a bit less time eating junk food with his thieving buddies. Carter had reported that TJ hardly brought the guys over lately. The textbook, too, seemed to suggest that TJ wanted something that had nothing to do with bad vodka and everything to do with building a future.

Still, Kristine knew it wasn't easy to fully change a teenager's mind. She wanted to be there to help Carter every step of the way if she could.

"Why don't we go to the dining hall?" Kristine suggested. "There's a killer burger place I've been dying to eat at all week long."

"What do you think, bud?" Carter asked.

TJ shrugged, trying to play it cool. "I could eat."

Together, the three of them walked from the parking lot, past the beautiful admission office, through a tree-lined garden, and finally, to the dining hall, where numerous students milled around, chatting and adjusting their backpacks over their shoulders. Kristine watched TJ's eyes as he studied the students curiously, perhaps even imagining himself as one of them.

"Maybe we could visit some other colleges across Maine together," Kristine suggested, excited about the prospect of helping this teenage boy find his way. "Every college is unique. Maybe you'll fall in love with the University of Maine or the University of Bangor."

In the dining hall, they ordered burgers, fries, and sodas from the kiosk and sat with their food, surrounded by swarms of students. When TJ got up to retrieve some ketchup, Carter whispered in Kristine's ear, "Thank you for this. Really. For years, TJ refused to even talk about college. Now that we're here together, I have hope for him. Maybe he'll find a way to really walk the right path."

"And maybe, once TJ is off building his life, you'll finally have time to think about what you want to be," Kristine breathed, her eyes widening.

Carter's cheeks burned red. After a small pause, he said, "It goes against every instinct I have to think about my own future."

Kristine squeezed his hand. "You've put everyone else first for too long."

"It's funny that falling for you means learning to like myself again," Carter said.

"I think that's what love should be," Kristine breathed. "How can you love someone else if you don't love yourself?"

Carter and Kristine locked eyes for a long time, both overwhelmed. At first, Kristine stung with fear for having said the "l-word," as they'd hardly dated at all. Then again, she truly believed she was falling for him in a very real way. Why shy away from something so true?

Just as TJ returned to the table, one of Kristine's professors, Professor McLear, passed by. Kristine waved, and Professor McLear paused for a moment, adjusting her tray against her stomach.

"Good evening, Kristine," she said, then nodded to both TJ

and Carter. "Thank you for all your hard work in my class so far. It can be difficult for a student to enter into a semester at the halfway point, but I'm happy to see you've taken it in stride."

Kristine blushed, overwhelmed at the compliment. "Thank you for saying that." She paused, then eyed TJ as he sat across from her. "This is my friend, TJ. He's thinking about where he wants to go to college and what he wants to study."

Professor McLear took this very seriously, showing TJ the utmost respect. "It's a very important question in a young person's life. The thing you have to remember most is this, though. No matter what you choose, you can always change your mind. Life is very long, and there are so many things to learn and discover. Keep yourself open to every possibility. Promise me that?"

TJ was caught off-guard. "Yes, ma'am."

"Good." Professor McLear nodded, locked eyes with Kristine, and said, "Have a beautiful night, you three." She then walked toward the back doorway and disappeared down the hallway.

That night, as TJ read his textbook in the backseat of the truck and Carter drove them back home, Kristine gazed out across the glow of Frenchman Bay and felt the warm breeze across her cheeks. The radio station played a love song she hadn't heard in decades, one that reminded her of her father and the way he'd loved her mother for all those years. How lucky she was to experience real love and all its mysticisms. How lucky she was to begin again.

Also by Katie Winters

Check out my new series:

The Copperfield House

Other Books by Katie

Connect with Katie Winters

Amazon
BookBub
Facebook
Newsletter

To receive exclusive updates from Katie Winters please sign up
to be on her Newsletter!
CLICK HERE TO SUBSCRIBE

Lightning Source UK Ltd.
Milton Keynes UK
UKHW020623210223
417374UK00010B/1029